The fire had made for itself a pocket of dryness and had gained strength. By the time the princess was roused and on her feet, the western wall of her room was charring and the women could hear the snaps of burning in the roof above them.

Lady Takumi dashed about, snatching up silk robes, piles of paper, fans, belts, hair ornaments, crying out "Oh! Oh! Oh!" at the thought that such gorgeous things might be burned. Finally she had so overburdened herself that the whole armful tumbled away to the floor and Lady Miyuki urged her through the door.

Lady Miyuki was new in the household. She was always watchful but inexpressive. Aoi was surprised to see, as she turned to lead the princess to safety in the front courtyard, that Lady Miyuki was smiling.

Smiling, with bright eyes, looking back to see flames burst out of the wall, watching the servants with their buckets at the edge of the pond, ducking under the blackness of the smoke, her face animated as Aoi had not yet seen it.

With a sudden flap and roar, the fire asserted its hunger and the women fled.

THE
EXILE WAY

ANN WOODWARD

AVON BOOKS ◆ NEW YORK

VISIT OUR WEBSITE AT
http://AvonBooks.com

THE EXILE WAY is an original publication of Avon Books. This work has never before appeared in book form. This work is a novel. Any similarity to actual persons or events is purely coincidental.

AVON BOOKS
A division of
The Hearst Corporation
1350 Avenue of the Americas
New York, New York 10019

Copyright © 1996 by Ann Woodward
Published by arrangement with the author
Library of Congress Catalog Card Number: 96-96427
ISBN: 0-380-78497-1

First Avon Books Printing: November 1996

AVON TRADEMARK REG. U.S. PAT. OFF. AND IN OTHER COUNTRIES, MARCA REGISTRADA, HECHO EN U.S.A.

Printed in the U.S.A.

RA   10 9 8 7 6 5 4 3 2 1

To Murasaki Shikibu, Sei Shonagon,
the Mother of Michitsuna,
and whoever it was who wrote the Eiga Monogatari

And to Edward G. Seidensticker,
Ivan Morris, and the McCulloughs,
whose remarkable scholarship has
voiced these Heian women's writings into English

Author's Note

This novel is set in Japan in the later years of the Heian Period, at the beginning of the Western eleventh century. Since the Japanese of that time used a lunar calendar and the year began not in what we call January but in early February, it should be kept in mind that the Fourth Month, for instance, is not April but May.

Pronunciation of Japanese vowels is simple and relatively unvarying. Here are equivalences: *a* as in *lark, i* as in *feel, u* as in *loot, e* as in *peck, o* as in *tone*. Each vowel is pronounced separately, as in Aoi (ah-OH-ee).

Prologue

The First Boy

The house was cold. Still, heavy cold pressed against the boy's skin as if it would pry apart every particle and invade the center. They had told him to wait in this bare room. Though his father had sent for him, some fresh emergency of his illness had caused the women to run through the halls carrying basins and cloths. He had not seen his mother for two days. His elder sisters would not leave their room and if he went to their door he would hear them weeping. His tutor had been sent away but he would have been impressed to see how the boy, left alone for so long a time in his room, had practiced writing to amuse himself.

When finally they fetched him to his father's side, the boy would not look at him but searched with his eyes for his mother. She was not there. "Soon I will be gone," he heard, as he was wondering where she was. He wanted to ask her for soup. He wanted to tell her that a mouse had sat for an instant in a corner of his room, looking straight at him.

1

"Pay attention," his father said. The boy bowed and gripped his hands on his knees, thinking how the icy polished boards on which he knelt radiated cold through the cloth of his three robes, thinking that the brazier at his father's feet did nothing to warm the floor.

"They will be good to you there," he heard.

"It is too cold in here," the boy said. "Why don't they bring you more braziers? You shouldn't be cold."

"I have worried about you," his father said. "You are so young. There are none of my family left to sponsor you and when I am gone there will be little income to support your entry into a good position in the government. Finally this has seemed the best solution."

You don't have to be ill, the boy was thinking. If they would get you warm you wouldn't cough so.

"The priest will come for you today." His father was wiping away tears with a corner of his sleeping robe.

"I am to leave?"

"Don't be sad. This is for your future. I want to go knowing you will be well taken care of."

The boy was led away. My mother won't let them do this, he thought. She will stop them. He asked for her and they said she was not well. He could hear her sobbing in her room across the hall.

When the priest came the boy was led to the door. "Where are my things?" he asked, seeing that there was not even the smallest box packed for him.

"You won't need them," said the maid who held his hand. "They will give you everything there." She too wiped tears from her cold cheeks, huddling her arms across her middle when the door opened.

Suddenly he understood that he was really being taken away and he screamed out. "I didn't mean to, I'm sorry, I'm sorry!" But what was it he had done?

The ox driver, a chubby young boy, helped him into the bare and shabby cart. Under the eye of the monk, the driver did not dare speak to the frightened child, but his hands lingered in comfort on his feet as he moved them aside to close the gate and he pressed his lips together to show that silence was best. The driver knew what it was to leave home, only in his case he had gladly gone from a house of poverty to the temple where he would have food twice a day. The boy, watching the verandah that was outside his mother's rooms and hoping she would show herself, did not see the pledge in the ox driver's look and probably would not have recognized the beginning of devotion and dedication.

In the carriage the cold was worse, cutting through every crack and opening. The monk who had charge of him said, "We must pray for your father." He held a string of carved wooden beads and he began to move his lips, slipping the beads through his fingers one by one.

I will not pray, the boy thought. Father did not have to be ill, they did not take care of him. And she could have kept me, he thought, but she wouldn't. He pulled open his robes and bared his chest to the cold air moving past him. Maybe if he let himself get cold enough he would die too. The monk thought how pious he was to punish his flesh for his father's sake.

The Second Boy

Weak, the old woman thought, the girl has always been weak. Would she have the strength to bear this child, screaming and sobbing through the whole day, her eyes blank with terror at the uncontrollable grip of her muscles? What can my son have seen in her, to raise her so high as royal concubine, to outrage all the court with his obsessive attentions?

Her women knew to keep away when the former empress knelt cross-armed and motionless behind her curtains. She had aged to thinness, her face was sallow and her graying hair coarse and unruly under a nun's headdress. If the girl's father still lived, she would be giving birth in his house. But both her parents had died in last year's epidemic, leaving their daughter with no influential backing to ward off the hostility of the emperor's wives and their ladies. Except that now they dare not, the old woman thought. She is mine now. When I let her go back—if I let her go back—they must think of me before they mistreat her.

Priests crowded the verandahs, chanting their prayers and spells. The wet nurse had come and gone again, claiming that she would lose her milk if she were to remain in such confusion. The girl's own women had collapsed under the retired empress's continuous and stern instructions that they raise their mistress from the bed pads or lower her, or give her hot magnolia-bark tea, or bathe her eyes, or hold her hands away from her hair lest she tear it out, and they had ended by running into the garden in tears, leaving a trio of callous and bulky nurses in charge. Extensions of the old woman's will, these three massaged and maneuvered with pitiless expertise.

The cries from the northern rooms climbed to new pitches and slid to new depths. The priests chanted more rapidly. Weak, weak, it will all be for nothing, the old woman was saying to herself into a sudden stillness. And there it was, the baby's cry. She gripped her hands together, making the prayer beads leap and click on the floor in front of her. Thin and uneven, the child's wail seemed about to stop, rose, fell, bumped past several breaths, and ran to an even keening. She did not notice, so grateful was she, the puny sound of it.

Still wiping her hands on a towel, the oldest of the nurses pulled aside the curtain, waddled on her knees to bow and sit at a distance from the old nun. "A boy," she said and watched startled pleasure bloom on the grandmother's face.

For months mother and child were both unwell. The retired empress prayed and she ordered the prayers of powerful priests. Her women wore themselves out, nursing the feverish mother and the child who could not find strength to scream but wailed and spat and fainted into nervous sleep. The wet nurse was dismissed, another took her place; but the child remained thin and fretful, unable to retain the milk so generously given. No one in the whole house could rest day or night, and the retired empress, hollow-eyed, grew more and more enraged with her son for his choice of this weakling of an orphan girl.

"I can do no more," she said finally one morning to the messenger who came several times a day with notes and inquiries from the emperor. "Tell him to prepare himself. Only a miracle can save them, I think." She wept, allowing herself the expression of sadness, though all she felt was bitter anger.

The emperor's man, a courtier of long experience and wide acquaintance, knew of the doctors, magicians, and famous priests who had been called in to help. He sat in quiet dejection, letting his shoulders fall, his head down, considering what he could say that would offer comfort. In the distant rooms of the mother, a medium screamed as a master exorciser tried to draw into her the evil spirits who were thought to be occupying the mother and her son. Arguments and the clang of pots could be heard from the kitchen, running feet thudded down the halls. There seemed to be no peace anywhere in the house. In contrast, he thought of the mansion of the Minister of the Right, which he had just left and which was noted for its harmony. At last, he thought, a new idea.

"My lady," he said, "why don't we ask the Minister of the Right if he knows of someone who could help. He seems to have a remarkable knack for acquiring talented servants."

The retired empress did not like mention of the Minister of the Right. One of her brothers was Minister of the Left and should have been the directing force in the government. But her brother was incompetent, spending his energy on ceremony and social affairs, and the Minister of the Right, though he made proper deference to the other, was the one who kept in his hands all the details of daily and long-range affairs, the one who was turned to for advice and planning.

The messenger soon took his leave, regretting an unwise suggestion. But after a few more days of the same ineffectual efforts to feed the baby, to cool the fever of the mother, the retired empress spoke to him again of his idea.

She did not greet him face to face, as her custom was with him, but had him brought to sit before her curtain screen, and her voice was offhand and uninterested as she said, "That pushy man you mentioned, he knows of our troubles?"

"Oh, my lady, you must realize that the whole country longs for health for this child and his mother." In fact the empress had been so anxious and concentrated in her concern that she had given no thought to widespread talk of the story of her son the emperor and his beloved concubine who was persecuted by jealous women. She was shocked and felt more than ever that somehow this situation must be solved, if only to let the story subside.

"Well, then . . ." Indirection was always her method and the messenger understood that he was to consult the Minister of the Right on her behalf. He understood also that, because she gave no explicit permission, he himself could be blamed if the minister's help turned out badly. Taking the risk, he went to the mansion of the competent Minister of the Right and waited until he returned from court.

So it was that the father of the princess whom Lady Aoi was later to serve as lady-in-waiting was given credit for saving the life of Prince Akimitsu and his mother. The women he sent, looked down upon by the retired empress and her household for their village air, had given the baby rice gruel, had begged for quiet in the house, had coaxed the mother to take soup and rice, had cooled her limbs and face, had opened the hushed rooms to the airs of spring, had rocked and soothed them both, and gradually the color and roundness of health had replaced their wanness. Disregarding his mother's resentment toward the minister, the emperor had rewarded him with an advance in rank and presents of sumptuous robes, articles of silver, bolts of brocade, and, most complimentary of all, frequent summonses for private visits. If the minister had not been such a modest man, all this attention from the emperor would have brought harmful jealousy. But he had threaded his way with his usual amused diffidence and had become even more influential.

Though the prince grew up healthy, the storms around him did not lessen. His grandmother kept him close all her life, insisting even after he was a good-sized boy that he sleep in her room.

"I won't have you running off to your mother, she is not well, you know that."

"Yes, but she is better when I come, she likes to see me, she says she is lonely."

"Let her be lonely, she has nothing for you, nothing for anyone. She can only weep and talk wild talk of being a prisoner. She does not know reality, she is not healthy, and she will bruise the flower of your soul and give you bad karma."

"My father asks for her still, he wants her at court."

"Your father had her at court in the days before, he does not appreciate the change in her. Come, we will do your lessons. Your calligraphy master has left this for practice, and you have not yet learned today's poems."

Calmly the child picked up the brush, wet the stone, ground the ink, loaded the badger's hair bristles full, and made broad strokes on his grandmother's cushion and the skirt of her outer robe. Looking her full in the face, he turned again to the inkstone, wet the brush, and flipped it to throw ink across the room and against the white paper of the sliding doors.

"Oh, oh, look what you have done! You must be more careful, my lovely boy, a brush is hard to handle. Hold it upright like this . . ." and another full brush met her correcting hand and smeared it black.

Anger choked in her throat and made her cheeks pale, her lips blue. "Well, let me see. Hasn't it been some time since you saw your mother? Why don't you visit her, you bad boy. You know she is always asking for you."

When the old empress died, mother and son were finally together. But the woman who had borne him could not keep him at his lessons, could not curb his temper or restrain him when he assaulted the servants. Finally the Minister of the Right was consulted again and he had to admit that the mother seemed too tentative and lax to cope with such a child and that, undisciplined as he was, he would become a danger as he matured. At age ten he was sent to relatives in the Province of Tamba. Aoi, who had just entered his daughter's household, happened to go with the minister on a gray day to see him off.

She remained in the carriage while the minister went inside to say goodbye and to try to quiet the mother's echoing cries of grief. After a long wait, she saw them emerge from the gallery and cross the courtyard to the boy's palanquin. She knew that it had been decided to take him in this luxurious way, not to honor him as son of an emperor but to keep a closer eye on him so that he could not jump down and run away.

Aoi had never seen this prince whose peculiarities were so well known. She thought him handsome, with strong features that showed his breeding. His hair, still cut in a boy's style, was so thick and abundant that his head seemed too large for the spindly body around which his rich clothes were bunched at the waist. He walked with pliance, wrists leading any motion of the arm, head leaning to one side or the other. Meekly enough he settled himself into the palanquin, one of his father's, and the minister spoke a few last words and closed the curtain.

As the men bore him through the gate, Aoi could see shreds appear in the yellow silk of the curtain. The boy was cutting it from inside with a sharp knife, strip after strip.

The Beginning of the Story
That Involves Them Both

It was dark when the men went in, making themselves part of the shadows of the pillars, their outlines so shagged and multilayered that they hardly looked human when clearly seen, and in the night were only moving clots of blackness. At first they had been frightened by the vastness around them. Bats and cobwebs they were used to but not so much space or such height of ceiling. To limit the press of emptiness, they had taken a corner for their meeting place and had made piles of straw-covered wine casks to further wall themselves in. There they could even use a light, a small oil lantern they had stolen and taken from its paper-covered frame. And there they fanned the bits of charcoal they would take away in boxes lined with metal.

"I don't understand who he is."

"Just hope you never find that out, it wouldn't be good for your health."

"But no one's ever seen him around. Just suddenly he puts out word to the stablehand and we're wooden-headed enough to meet him. It would make anyone laugh."

"The stablehand isn't laughing at us when we take him so much good stuff to sell."

"Unh. Soon I'll have enough gold to bribe the guards at the barrier, and then I'm running for the north. They give away whole farms up there, if you clear the fields yourself."

"If things go on like this, you'll have your farm. But I don't trust him."

"Why do you say that? He's just like us."

"Seems so. But he smells."

"Little brother, you make me tired. The man got hold of incense somewhere—and so he smells better than us."

"He doesn't talk like we do."

"As one who has served in a lord's house, I can tell you that he probably has a position in a nice place and he is used to polite speech. Of course, he shouldn't waste it on yokels like you, since you distrust anyone who talks polite to you."

"What does he do with those things he hides under the cloth? And how does he always know where we'll find them?"

"When your tongue is ripped out, will it still ask questions, little brother? You do remember, little brother, a talkative man we know . . .?"

"Put out the light! There's someone . . ."

Footsteps could be heard on the sanded walk outside. One dark figure moved around the casks to see who it was. Several ladies-in-waiting were passing, their robes fluttering and glimmering in the darkness. The man inside stood near the doorway and began a soft chittering murmur, giggling and smacking his lips. The women ran screaming.

"Little brother," said one of the others when he returned to the corner, "you do make a very good ghost."

Chapter 1

"My lady, there are more of those priests ahead, they block the main gate. We will turn here and take you to the Koga Gate instead."

"Yes," Aoi answered. All her view was banded by the slender strips of the closed blind. The ox paced around the corner to the left and the carriage entered a narrow street lined with the walls of residential compounds. In sudden quiet, the grinding sounds of the wheels and the steps of the horses of her three outriders were loud. Rioting priests still shouted in the distance, their threats and the knocking of their staves on the wood of the gates damping to a roar, the voice of confused times.

Here at the end of the Ninth Month the harvest was in and the weather still warm. The mountain priests, always belligerent and dissatisfied and now free of field work for a while, had come down to the city in their brown robes to threaten the government. Chasing the carriage of an official, they had passed her on Suzaku Avenue and she had thought, I will not let myself become used to this, I will not think it normal for men to make these raging sounds. She reminded herself that because the rule of the Law of the Buddha was fading into the prophesied decadent age, it was important to hold on to a sense of normal civilized standards.

There were no guards at the Koga Gate, they had all run to counter the priests at the Suzaku Gate. She was a little relieved. She always saw the sly looks when she stepped down from the carriage, a lone woman arriving at dusk and walking into the inner grounds. The outriders knew that she preferred to go alone, hoping to pass as a simple woman of the court on a simple errand and not a lady who would soon be in the emperor's presence. The walkways were paved with coarse white sand, bright even in darkness, and she did not need a man to come with her and light the way.

Because she had arrived at a side gate, her path to the emperor's residence took her along the wall that enclosed the old Court of Abundant Pleasures. In failing light the crumbling wall and the sedge roof beyond with weeds growing at its edges looked mellow and antique. This hall, never used now, was said to be haunted. She imagined that the music and poetry of a past age still echoed among the lofty pillars inside, as if the calm strength of peace and order collected in the places where they had been most intense. On impulse, she turned through an opening in the wall.

The garden was rough with ungoverned growth, an ancient pine drooped its branches low across the path, once-rounded shrubs grew together, spiky and uneven, and the paths were littered with sticks, fallen cones, and dead leaves. She raised her hand to move aside a pine branch but stilled her arm because the building spoke.

She thought first of bats and they were indeed cutting great arcs through the evening air, but silently. The sound that had come from the hall had been a soft chittering tone sliding from high to low. Darkness seemed to close to ground level as the voice descended. When it rose to begin another cascade, footsteps drummed across board floors and in the very last of the the light she saw a couple run down the steps with a tearing brush of cloth against moving legs.

Lovers, she thought. But they had not made the strange sound she had imagined was the voice of the old building, a sound that was not attractive and did not fit with her idea of echoing past culture. About to lift the pine branch and proceed, she hesitated. Then, I am expected, she thought, and she turned back, walked on toward the center of the grounds, past the long row of buildings set into a hill on the left, where the highest ministers had their offices, past the well, and, turning right, to the imperial residence. She mounted the steps and was met by a chamberlain. From a nearby room came sounds of the muted conversation of officials who waited, even this late in the day, to be admitted to the royal presence. They were never received after sundown but they always lingered until the last moment. The chamberlain had put them in the small room so that Aoi could pass into the interior hall unobserved. The emperor waited inside the raised and curtained enclosure in the center of a large hall.

"The Lady Aoi has arrived," the chamberlain said, holding aside a white curtain.

Except for the chamberlain who had greeted her, all his attendants had been sent away and he was alone, a sturdy man with graying hair. He had never thought to be emperor. An older brother had succeeded to the throne years ago and another brother was made crown prince. Without specific official duties, he had lived comparatively freely, serving in those government posts that interested him, hunting and hawking as other men did, but also indulging his taste for Chinese history and collecting and studying the tales of travelers on the continent. Then, when he had reached his thirties, there had been an epidemic and the emperor died, the crown prince died, and he was left almost the only male in the royal family. So it was with surprise but a sense of fitness and readiness that he had become emperor five years ago. An emperor was usually a prisoner of ceremony, but because of his maturity and experience, and because the ministers respected his judgment, this emperor took an unusually strong role in government affairs. Now he was less and less able to read and to keep up with daily details, and Aoi had heard that some councillors were saying that he should resign. The crown prince was a boy of sixteen whose laziness and fondness for sport and games were a source of bitterness to his father.

She bowed and murmured formal greetings.

"Lady, you are good to come every day like this. It is inconsiderate of me, asking you to arrive in near darkness, but . . ." His voice died away, as it often did now.

"No, no. People talk so much that it is best not to give them a new subject. The palace doctors distrust any treatments not their own and they would be very critical if they knew that I come here. And yet this—" She took a fold of cloth from under her belt and began to unwrap it. "The use of blue vitriol for the infection that afflicts you is clearly advised in many ancient Chinese treatises on medicine," and she spread the cloth on the floor beside her, arranging small blue crystals in a row. The chamberlain brought a lantern and set it near the emperor, then left the enclosure. He would guard the door until Aoi was ready to leave.

"The doctors are too cautious. When a man suffers as I do, then they should try everything. But they retreat into spells and magic and I only become more miserable."

"They have a great responsibility and not one of them dares differ from the others. I think it is because these crystals come from copper that they refuse to try them—any metallic compound reminds them of Taoist medicines, which are often lethal. This one, though, I have used many times or I would not have dared treat Your Highness with it."

"It is certain that I am better now. Your touch of blue, as you call it, is helping. Though I do not look forward to the touch itself, the inflammation is soothed afterward and I am able to rest all night." His voice faded again and he glanced toward her. She had put slender wooden chopsticks on the cloth and she waited. He sighed, preparing himself for necessary pain. "You are ready then . . ."

Taking the crystals one by one and discarding them into a paper cone, Aoi touched and lifted, touched and lifted until every spot of intruding growth was treated. The used crystals would be buried in the ground, as the Chinese doctors advised. He stood it without a sound. "Be sure that a fresh cloth is prepared for each day's bandage," she said, tying a white band about his eyes. "I will remind the chamberlain."

"Ah." He made an impatient gesture. "Why am I so afflicted? My life has been too pleasant, I expected to continue to be lucky. But all the time this awful karma of illness waited to reveal itself. It is not possible to examine the past of all the previous lives I can't remember, but what disturbs me is that I don't know if I have done bad things in this life. I try to tell myself that I did not covet my brother's position. Yet after a while I could see what he should have been doing and perhaps I wanted to take his place, to become emperor myself. And I did not offer to help."

"You know that your brother was strong-headed and would not have accepted your help."

"Don't comfort me, lady, in that way. I am most miserable because my pride will not let me find any fault in myself, though this disease must be a punishment. I have tried not to love my position. Yet if I am to have any effect at all, I must protect myself and keep my prerogatives, hold myself in some strength above all others. Saying that is to admit to pride and desire, don't you think? And so I shouldn't wonder about the origin of bad karma in a previous life, there is plenty of origin here in my present life."

"Good acts are a force in the world as well as bad acts, and a good man can restrain bad men, as you have no doubt done throughout your rule. Can't you see your disease as an accident unrelated to the way you have lived? It will be cured by this blue medicine. Let the pain of the cure be your trial and when you are healthy again in your body, you will come into spiritual peace."

"Health is a blessing, you are right. But for many years I was unimpaired and did not think of it as a positive thing. Now that I am nearly blind, I see my past blindness and the sin of it. I feel the need to heal my soul but I am afraid that if I leave . . ." Turning his head, he seemed to be listening to the distant shouts of the priests.

They had had this conversation many times and Aoi knew that the emperor would not accept any reassurances at all. She could only hope that his spirits would improve as his eyes pained him less.

Her cloth and the crystals, now enclosed in paper, were tucked back into her belts and she took her leave. Outside the door she meant to speak to the chamberlain but a man approached from down the corridor and Aoi turned away toward the entrance, keeping as near the wall as she could. The man was a member of the Great Council of State and she heard him say, "Who is that leaving His Majesty's room? It looks like that woman who is always mixing medicines for people. You shouldn't let such a dangerous person near the emperor. Who appointed you? Haven't you any sense at all?"

Aoi had heard many ignorant and slighting comments in her life and she tried to avoid people who would find it necessary or amusing to ridicule a learned woman. If confronted, she never answered. She knew that the testimony of those cured or relieved would always be her defense. In this case, though, the emperor's cure depended on her access to him and she moved in the deepest shadows as she left the hall.

In the distance the priests still shouted and thumped on the Suzaku Gate. The Court of Abundant Pleasures was silent as she passed. Outside the smaller gate, her carriage waited to take her back to the house of the princess.

Chapter 2

In the humid air of the Ninth Month smoke does not rise. It lingers and spreads low, sidles along behind drafts, and palely wafts apart. Lit only briefly by secret flames, gray smoke in the gray light before dawn slides ungathered to the floor and hovers there. The receiving air, soft with mist, expands each particle of carbon as it escapes, the least scent of which will alarm those who live in wooden houses.

Aoi was asleep when the first odor of fire reached her, and she woke already half-sitting, eyes still closed, lungs filling with small breaths. Was it smoke? Or had her sense of smell responded to a dream? In this hot weather she did not sleep well, her dreams were of trouble and unease. She lay down again, still testing the air. Not smoke. She almost dozed.

Aoi slept in a small room next to the apartment of the princess. Because she was senior, she did not share her place as did the other three ladies-in-waiting, who slept together in the adjoining larger room. Beyond the space where the princess slept—on a pallet laid on a woven straw platform and enclosed by four-foot damask curtains hung on standing frames—was a private room for her husband the prince, who was this night, as on many nights, not in residence.

From the prince's room the smoke leaked into the corridor, the particles of it crowding now, and Aoi was startled fully awake by certainty and urgency. She stood, to move around and try to tell how strong the smoke smell was and how close. Just the week before a house had burned in the next avenue, a much grander house than this simple one the princess had taken for herself. And it had begun, they said, at just this time of early morning, when everyone still slept. On that morning the wind had blown the fire from roof to roof and several mansions and their compounds had been destroyed. Knowing that this incident was still in her mind, Aoi did not want to trust too easily her sleeping impression of danger.

She opened the sliding door and leaned into the corridor. The smell of smoke was stronger here, but still she could not tell if it came from inside the house or if it swelled in with the outside air of the garden. She stepped around the fine bamboo blind that separated the corridor from the verandah beyond. Because of the unseasonable hot weather, the outside shutters had been left open and for a moment she stood looking at the dimmed, grayed shapes of shrubs and trees in the garden, the hazed surface of the pond, the blotches of color where flowers bloomed. There was no sound, it was too early even for the kitchen servants to be at their work, the birds were not yet calling.

And will you stand here while the house burns down? she said to herself, stand here caught by this scene of enclosed perfection, thinking how lucky to be the one awake to see it, distilling poetry? In fact the beginning of a poem had already formed.

> *Alone with itself,*
> *The garden . . .*

Impatient with this familiar weakness for things of the world, she broke the custom of thought that would have cast her feeling into ordered form, but she knew that this phrase would always bring back to her the purified shapes and clear design of the princess's garden in pale light.

One flash of movement caught her eye and she looked across to the opposite side just in time to see a broad-heeled bare foot completing its step past the gap between two blinds. On that side was the prince's room. Had he come in during the night? But that foot, knobbed and spread, had been no princely foot.

Intruders.

Her impulse was to run toward the prince's room but she stopped before she had more than shifted her shoulders forward. And there was smoke, she could see it now threading through the blind where the foot had passed. She bent slightly to soften her outline and eased backward until the blind behind her slipped aside and let her pass again into her room. Then she ran.

A simple rattle of the sliding doors was enough to wake the others. Lady Omi answered at once.

"Yes?"

"Wake up. There is fire, we must get the princess out." And now, Aoi decided, it was time to make noise. If there were robbers in the house, only commotion and numbers of people would frighten them away. "Call the servants!" she shouted, shrinking at the unaccustomed loudness of her voice. She could hear Lady Takumi begin to wail inside the room, just as Aoi had expected she would. Before anyone could call her, Aoi's maid O-hana came running. One look from Aoi and O-hana understood everything: that fire had been set in the house, that the fire setters were still about, that the carriage men and the cooks and maids were needed, that Aoi and the ladies would take care of the princess. O-hana turned and ran back the way she had come.

By now the fire had made for itself a pocket of

dryness and had gained strength. The straw platform suddenly blazed up against a curtain screen, which fell into a pile of writing paper on the desk, which, antique and dry, burned with heat against the inner wall, which smoldered into the rafters. Soon the old dry thatch was aflame and smoke rolled black into the lightening sky. By the time the princess was roused and on her feet, the western wall of her room was charring and the women could hear the snaps of burning in the roof above them.

The princess was calm, controlling her alarm and her distress at the damage to her house. She began to indicate to Lady Omi what robe she would wear but at a touch from Aoi turned away and tied up the clothes she had been sleeping in, moving at the same time toward the door. Lady Takumi dashed about, snatching up silk robes, piles of paper, fans, belts, hair ornaments, crying out "Oh! Oh! Oh!" at the thought that such gorgeous things might be burned. Finally she had so overburdened herself that the whole armful tumbled away to the floor and Lady Miyuki urged her through the door.

Lady Miyuki was new in the household. If she had been impressed by the level of society she entered when her relatives spoke for her to the princess and she had taken the place of a lady who married and moved away, she covered any display of it with indifference and an air of almost boredom. She was always watchful but inexpressive. Aoi was surprised to see, as she turned to lead the princess to safety in the front courtyard, that Lady Miyuki was smiling, helping Lady Takumi retrieve a few of the princess's luxuries, pulling her away from the rest, and finally pushing her from behind. Smiling, with bright eyes, looking back to see flames burst out of the wall, watching the servants with their buckets at the edge of the pond, ducking under the blackness of the smoke, her face animated as Aoi had not yet seen it.

With a sudden flap and roar, the fire asserted its hunger and the women fled.

Chapter 3

Wearing their oldest clothes, which were what they used for sleeping, dirty with soot and light-headed from shock, the women went to the house of the Great Minister of the Right, who was the princess's father. They refused to separate or to rest, and the minister, fearing eventual hysteria, stayed at home to calm them.

Lady Takumi had not once stopped her crying. Lady Omi and Lady Aoi, being older, were quiet, but Aoi was aware of a deep quaver below her ribs and kept her hands pressed there. Lady Miyuki locked and unlocked her fingers and watched the princess, who had forced herself to stillness, as usual. The princess's face was pale, her eyes stared, and while the others talked for relief, she said nothing. When finally she spoke in almost a whisper, her question silenced them all.

"Where is he?"

"He is coming. I have sent word," said the minister.

"He should have been with me."

"Yes." The minister stirred and sighed. "Yes,

he . . ." The futility of giving voice to the prince's shortcomings stopped him and he sighed again. "A man is as he is."

"Do you excuse him, then, Father?"

"No, no. I only see that he doesn't change. You know I have never accepted the way he treats you. But there is no influence, it seems . . ."

What they all knew was that the prince probably could not have been found on such short notice. He had several wives, who did not all live in his large mansion, and many other interests among women, whom he was likely to visit for a night. The princess was his principal wife, an honor even neglect could not dim, but honor did not satisfy her. Most women in her position would have lived with their fathers, even after marriage. But Aoi's princess felt too keenly the shame of her jealous outbursts to let her father see them, and had chosen privacy for her struggles.

So it was to her father and not to her husband that neighboring servants had run, it had been the Great Minister of the Right and not the prince who came with three carriages, racing his oxen, skidding the high wheels around corners, to take her and her women away from the ruined house. They had been finally forced to stand in the street, the princess shielded from view by her ladies, by the fan she never lowered in public, and by one of Aoi's robes held above her head. Knowing how she disliked being seen by strangers, the minister had ordered the back gate of his carriage opened at once and helped her up beside him into the padded and brocaded interior almost before the runners had steadied the stepping stool. Aoi too he had motioned in, the others went to the two carriages behind, with the servants and a great pile of articles rescued from the house. Aoi relaxed when, looking back, she saw that O-hana had her box of scrolls and medicines. Then they had sat to watch for a while through bamboo screens as the western wing of the house burned. Lady Takumi wailed the whole time, as if she had forgotten to stop.

At one point there was an outcry from the servants when they saw two unknown men run behind the shrubs of the garden and heave themselves over the wall. The minister did not tell them until later that the method in such robberies was to set a fire in some part of a house, then go into the private rooms as they were vacated by the fleeing occupants, tie up valuables in large cloths, and drop the bundles to a partner outside the walls, to be hidden at once under a load of vegetables or in a fish cart and taken away. The police never caught these men. It was only conjecture from the evidence of stains and debris on the few articles that were dropped or discarded that gave them the way it was done.

Seeing his daughter compress her lips and turn away at what he had said about the prince, the minister clucked in his throat, glanced at Aoi, and said again, "A man is as he is." He meant not only that he himself tended toward tolerance but that the prince found pleasurable response from many women and complaining would not change his needs.

Lady Omi said, "How quickly you came. You must have been up and dressed already."

"I always meet early with the other minister's secretary and we get things settled before the petitioners arrive."

"And the Great Minister of the Left, does he too rise early?" asked Lady Takumi. The man often called "the other minister" held the primary position in the government as Minister of the Left, the emperor having awarded it to him because of the eminence of his family. Everyone knew that he gave his share of the details of governing to the princess's father, who held the second position.

"It is necessary that the other minister save his energy. You have no idea how he works, enduring all those ceremonies and banquets—and since he often stands in for me their number is great. He probably gets very little sleep, up doing his duty half the night, required to drink cup after cup of wine. Simply disposing of his headaches is a full-time job." The minister's serious geniality did not falter and Lady Takumi hid her teasing smile, raising her wrist and pulling the edge of her sleeve across the lower half of her face.

Lady Miyuki had lapsed back into her expression-less mode, sitting with head bent slightly away, her long hair dropping across her cheek. Whatever had caused her liveliness when they escaped the fire, she had then for the first time shown the attractiveness of intelligence and interest. Now she was aloof and guarded again and she did not join the conversation.

The minister lived in the kind of mansion typical of the homes of the nobility. It was in the Second Ward, not far from the palace enclosure, in the northeast corner of the city. Here in the rising foothills, pro-tected from the fierce demons of the north by moun-tains, spacious walled compounds lined the avenues, each one enclosing many buildings connected by roofed corridors, each with a winding stream that passed under the passageways and formed a lake in the garden. All the main halls faced south, to catch the prevailing breeze in summer, the low sun in winter, and all opened completely to the gardens in hot weather, when the rain shutters were hooked onto the ceilings of the verandahs and only thin-stripped blinds hid the interiors. Polished floorboards stretched throughout, almost unbroken by inside walls. Private space was made with folding screens and curtain stands, comfort for sitting and sleeping was provided by cushions and straw mats.

Aoi, looking at the garden scene finely textured by the green bamboo blind, felt the contentment she always knew when she came to this mansion with her mistress. The princess was calmer here, less bitter toward her husband, less strict with herself in trying to impose outer calm no matter what her feelings were. As now she allowed herself tears.

"Oh Father, my house is gone, I cannot joke about the other minister."

"Well now, we certainly do not joke about the fire at your house, but what would life be without jokes about the other minister? And your house is damaged but it is not by any means gone. It will just take a few months to repair it, I have already sent to my estates for carpenters and thatchers. In the meanwhile you will visit me, with your charming companions, and we shall enjoy together this last pleasant warmth. One needs company in the evenings, when it is too warm to go to bed. That is the time for conversation, for music and fireflies, and I have missed these things since you left."

Though the princess would not so easily give up her tears, she relaxed her posture and cried without tension, almost happily, so pleased was she to have her situation made a matter of practical remedy and so glad of an excuse to be in this house for a while.

The princess's servants were all sent home to visit their families. O-hana joined Aoi and behaved very queerly for an hour and a half, until Aoi forced her to say what the trouble was.

"Oh my lady, your box . . ."

"Not my box. But I saw you bring it out to the carriage."

"Yes, I brought it. It is not the box. That is, not the whole box. They couldn't take it, it was too big, I suppose . They could hardly tie—"

"O-hana."

"But the medicine chest . . ."

"They took that? They went *into* my box and took the little chest from it?" How long would it take her, Aoi thought, to replace the treasures in that medicine chest with its little drawers: the ginseng from Silla, the musk, orpiment, sulphur, ocher, minium, wolfbane. Where would she find again aconite like that given to her by an old priest who had visited the continent in his youth? Fine Chinese spiky niter had been in that chest, cinnamon, cloves, gallnuts, licorice, and pepper for seasoning and for clearing the spirit, realgar to counteract poisons, yu gold and fritillary, ox bezoar and cassia bark. And most importantly, blue vitriol for treating the emperor's eyes.

The main content of the larger box had been her collection of scrolls. She did not dare ask O-hana about them but she looked so distressed that the maid quickly said, "No, no. The scrolls are there. That is, most of them. That is, I think they may have taken one or two."

The thieves must have gone immediately into the rooms the women had left. That box of scrolls with its small chest of medicines in one corner was Aoi's greatest treasure. O-hana, on the morning of the fire, had run first to call the carriage men and then straight to the scroll box to take it to safety in the garden.

When the box was brought to her, blackened by smoke but otherwise unharmed, Aoi lifted out the scrolls and bound books of paper, some of them quite old, some in protective covers. She ran down the mental list of what should be there: Here was the scroll with excerpts from the T'ao Hung-ching, here was the account of Chinese physicians and their most notable cures. The famous dietary recipes of Sun were safe, and the little book of copies from an illustrated catalog of herbs. Rolls and rolls of her own notes were there, tied up with cord as she always kept them. The scroll of her father's poems and paintings was untied and a little ripped beside the lacquered spine at the beginning. One elaborately bound scroll that had been a gift from her friend the empress had had its knobs of gold and rock crystal ripped from the ends of the spool. Missing were the two that had been the most sumptuously covered—which were ancient notes from the records of the Chinese emperor's herb gardener and a simple picture scroll done by a famous Japanese calligrapher of the past century. A copy of the treatise on diseases of the eye by Sun Szu-miao was also gone, though it had been only a paper scroll with a simple silk cover. All were valuable beyond cost and irreplaceable.

Most women could not read Chinese, but Aoi's

father had taught her, against custom. He had been a teacher and scholar and he had not been able to resist his only child's eagerness to study. As she grew she had learned many things from her reading but she had come to concentrate on the useful knowledge of Chinese medicine. Such unwomanly learning was often ridiculed by those who wished to spite Aoi, but her skills in diagnosis and healing, her ability to soothe with massage, her calm and practical help when someone was sick, and her carefully administered medicines were appreciated, though her successes only made her all the more envied and resented by the small-minded.

Aoi felt diminished by the loss of these resources of power against physical ills. She was a woman who treated and healed, but this part of her identity did not lie entirely in her memory. Without references and medicines she lost width of experience and effectiveness. For the first time she realized fully the value of her education, of those hours spent memorizing Chinese letters, practicing with the writing brush, searching through scrolls often tedious and obscure, for the truth of other people's experience and observation.

It was particularly bad luck that the scroll on eye diseases was gone, because she had often needed that scroll in recent weeks. Though she was using the blue vitriol exactly as Sun prescribed, care was needed and she had referred again and again to Sun's work.

Now the blue vitriol was gone too, and she was not sure she could replace it. Her original supply had come long ago from an old pharmacist who always said that the palace doctors practiced a form of magic to protect themselves when they could not cure. He had admired Aoi's willingness to admit ignorance as well as her wide knowledge and he had always been able to procure unusual ingredients for her. Did that old man still live, and could she find him?

Soothing O-hana, Aoi began to plan the restocking of her store of medicines. She was called back to other problems by the noises of the prince arriving at the main gate to comfort his wife. Leaving the box, Aoi went to help the princess into one of the new robes just sent from the Office of the Palace Wardrobe.

She found the princess in her room with the other ladies, who were offering her pots of lip rouge and boxes of white face powder, straightening her outer robe and combing her hair, which fell in a long stream of black onto the floorboards. They had dressed her in only two layers of thin robes, because of the heat. She was complaining that the new material was stiff, that the pink color of the top robe was too pretty for her situation as a woman who had barely escaped a bad fire, that her fan smelled of smoke and she must have a new one, and finally that her husband should not see her in such a condition.

"If he had been with me, I would not have thought of how I looked to him. This is a thing we should have shared. Yet there I was with only women in the house while criminals from the western city walked among us."

Aoi listened for a while to this, moving quietly to help with the dressing. If she allows herself tears, Aoi thought, it will be all right. But if she hardens, there will be long trouble.

The princess, turning her shoulders, moving her arms, was trying to accustom herself to the starched gauze of her new clothes. She moved toward the door, then turned back and indicated to Lady Takumi a wrinkle in the left sleeve. The wrinkle could not be smoothed, it was pressed in.

"This is impossible. What can those people be thinking of, to send me such a robe," and her searching anger found a focus. "I cannot be seen like this, as if no one cared for my clothes, as if I had no idea how to put myself together," and she ripped off the robe and turned away from them all. "Go and tell him that I cannot see him."

Lady Miyuki showed again a face of bright interest. Lady Takumi was sympathetic but dared not express

it. The princess, at these times, resented any indica-
tion that she was not in command of herself and of
the situation. Lady Omi was already offering another
robe, this one light yellow to go over the first robe,
which was green, but the princess let them both fall to
the floor and sat down in only her white under-robe
and pleated trousers. All of the ladies stepped back to
leave Aoi nearest the door and the one to carry the
message of refusal to the prince. Knowing from
experience that protest would only set the princess
more firmly against her husband, Aoi bowed, slid
open the door, and stood to walk through the cool
corridor to the main hall.

The day had darkened, thin streamers of cloud had
blown in on a mild breeze. She felt her clothes, still
the ones she had worn when they came here, wrap less
closely as she moved into the stirring air. Crossing the
bridge over the garden stream, she glanced at the
water where it raised white froth behind a stone set
near the bank.

> *Old stone, new water*
> *Breaking into old pattern,*
> *Change that does not change—*
> *Only more depth brings smooth flow,*
> *Only less can free the stream.*

Chapter 4

". . . that I was not at home," the prince was saying as
Aoi approached, "and so the message had to be
relayed. Life is very uncertain but who could have
expected this?"

"Ah, yes," said the minister, "that is unexpected-
ness for you—an arrow from the side."

"Sir, you tease me. Ah—" He broke off when he
saw Aoi. She bowed and knelt at a little distance.
Seeing the prince preparing to rise and go with her to
the princess, Aoi bowed again.

"Please do not disturb yourself. I am only a messenger." She bowed once more to hide her embarrassment.

"I see," he said. Aoi still kept her bow. She did not
need to look. He would have understood at once the
rebuff from his wife implicit in Aoi's seated presence.
But here before her father his face would put on an
expression first of puzzlement, then hurt, and finally
apprehension. "She was not injured?" and he started
up. Aoi was ashamed for him, for her mistress, and
for herself, that she must take a role in this pretense.

31

"No, no. She is perfect in her body. But she is upset," and Aoi subsided into sympathetic and consoling vagaries, murmuring, ". . . shock . . . seeing the walls afire . . . stumbling out just in time."

"Of course, of course." But his anger was not so easily tamped down. "I have come to hear these things from her. If she is terrified and upset, it is I who will—"

"But," interrupted the minister, "it was very early this morning that she was terrified. You are too late to protect her."

The prince closed his mouth and turned his head to one side, as if to release the force of his frustration in a safe direction. He was a handsome man, dressed today in a court costume of blue and yellow-green. His hair was tightly bound up into a knot under the black lacquered gauze cap that was proper for court wear, his face cleanly shaved and pale-skinned. Though he could be so slighted by his principal wife, he worked responsibly as a Major Councillor. His wives might number a few more than the normal for a nobleman, and his affairs with young ladies-in-waiting and other unmarried girls might be more widely known than those of other men, but his competence, his modest self-regard, the genuine attention and interest in his manner toward others made him respected in the whole city.

There had been times in the past when, so refused the company of his wife in punishment for some violation of her many standards for him, the prince would have pounded on the gates or shouted past her women to force his way into her room. Then the princess would be coldly silent, restraining the servants from letting him in, or if the violence of his presence came too close, she would cry out and cower until he left in disgust. Since their ardent courtship, times of attunement had been rare.

The prince bowed to the minister and to Aoi and prepared to leave, taking breath to voice loudly his disappointment and outrage that his wife had secluded herself."

"Stay awhile," said the minister. "Let Lady Aoi tell you about it. She was the one who woke them all."

The decision then for the prince was either to leave in anger, making a scene that would be heard all the way into the eastern wing where the princess was, or to give up dramatizing his feelings and hear what he most desired to know. He smiled, admitting his helplessness in this and any other aspects of his life that might, in this house, be held against him. Tension cleared and Aoi began, "I thought I had dreamed of fire."

When she had told it all—the suspicion of smoke, the sight of it coming through the blind of the prince's room (here he groaned and pulled his hands down across his face), the leap of her nerves when she saw a misshapen bare foot step past the blinds, the admirable calm of the princess as she was made to understand the threat, and the flight of all the ladies just ahead of the flames—the prince did not waste time saying, "Wah! How terrible!" as many would have done. Instead he spoke seriously of the sinister detail of the foot of the intruder. "This indeed I do not like," he said. "That they entered the house and went who-knows-where among sleeping women. If their intention had been murder and not distraction and robbery, they could have killed you all. I am afraid it was most unwise to leave the rain doors open."

"Yes. This is the third fire and robbery in a month," the minister said. "We are trying to concentrate the police in the northeast wards where they have all happened. The Palace Guards have been asked to help but they give us pious excuses and will not go outside the walls. They patrol the palace grounds in squads now, which gives thinner protection than ever."

The prince was considering. "Three fires and robberies in so short a time. Are they all—"

"Yes, similar. Early morning, fire and smoke to

make the inhabitants run to a remote part of the house or to safety outside. Then they go in and strip the rooms."

"And are the stolen articles seen for sale in the western part of the city?"

"Not yet. That puzzles us, because usually these thieves want only gold, knives, iron tools, or rice chits, they put no value on the things themselves, thinking only of exchange. And yet, you know what it is like over there in the west, the markets are hidden in stables, the backs of shops, private houses. Even if we could persuade the guards and the police to risk a raid, we would find nothing."

"Yes. Escaped farmers, criminal younger sons, and dismissed servants always hide in the western wards. They know they are safe there."

"In the case of my daughter's house," said the minister, "there was no particular collection or well-known valuable to take, but in all of the other cases the best art and scrolls and the most sumptuous robes were stolen. Could someone be informing them?"

"That is a serious thought. Ah, well. In this decadent age . . ." The prince sighed and bowed, preparing to depart. Aoi escorted him to the door and down the corridor to the place where his horse was held by one of the men who rode with him, and he left. Just as he reached the gate, he found some reason to laugh, making his voice sound, knowing his wife would hear and hoping she would think him unconcerned that she had kept herself from him.

Aoi covered her face by raising her left wrist in its smoke-stained sleeve. She turned her back before he was out of sight.

"O-hana," Aoi said when she was back in her room. "Did the wardrobe people send any clothes for us? I must cleanse myself of the smell of smoke, though until I can wash my hair——" She broke off as O-hana opened the door to speak to a maid who had knocked.

"There are visitors," O-hana said when she returned, and she unfolded and hung up one of Aoi's own robes, which she had saved from the fire. "I said you would come soon."

Hot water in a bronze basin was ready, and fresh under-robes. With O-hana's help Aoi washed and dressed. Last thing before putting on the waiting robe, she had the maid comb spirits of camphor through her hair, which they lifted and spread until it was dry for almost its whole length, and fragrant.

When finally she returned to the main hall, it was to find the minister and the princess entertaining a circle of acquaintances who had come to sympathize and to hear the story of their escape. Lady Omi had not yet changed clothes and she excused herself when Aoi appeared. Lady Takumi was wearing a robe much too gorgeous for such a simple occasion and Aoi could hear her explaining with an overly modest smile that it was the only one of her own that had been brought. The princess wore the pink robe she had discarded before, which showed only a small edge under her curtain.

Throughout the afternoon they told and retold the story. Lady Miyuki also had not changed from her smoke-stained robes. When the minister several times pointed out her condition as evidence of the serious-ness of the fire and the danger the women had escaped, she was quiet as usual but in a pleasant and smiling way. Every guest declared himself cautioned and said that he would go home to put a man on night guard duty and insist that all the shutters be closed tightly when the family retired, regardless of the heat. Every visitor also asked discreet questions about the prince, and it so irritated the princess to explain over and over that he had not been in the house during the fire that she very soon offended her guests and they left. The princess went to rest. Lady Miyuki and Lady Takumi, swaying a little too much to show off her embroidered satin, attended her. Aoi stayed behind to speak to the minister.

"I am worried and don't quite know what to do. Usually at the end of the day I visit the emperor to treat his eyes but . . ."

"You must go as usual, of course. Something as important as that treatment must not be interrupted."

"The trouble is, my medicine chest was stolen."

"Unh?"

"Yes, and I have no futher supply. I wonder . . . Could you send a message for me?"

"This is very distressing. His Majesty has told me that only you can give him relief with your—I believe he calls it, rather mysteriously, your touch of blue." The minister looked carefully at her face. "Now, now. So much anger will make you ill."

"No, I am only afraid it will make me weep. Such an unlucky chance, that someone thought a small box of many drawers must hold common valuables. But they are uncommon and valuable only to a person who knows how to use them. I had a life's supply of that medicine—one does not use much of it—but I am not sure I can get more."

"I see." The minister looked thoughtful.

"Should I go myself and try to explain?"

"You are more tired than you know. Let me do it for you. I was about to leave. But you must rest now and tomorrow you can begin your search."

Before they could rise from their cushions, another visitor was announced and came bowing into the hall. It was the other minister.

"I have heard," he said, "I have heard of your daughter's misfortune. My, my, how terrible," and he settled his round bulk on a cushion, patting the folds of his trousers into graceful lines, smoothing the rich fabrics of his several collars, and opening his court fan to pass it languidly before his face. There was a space of silence, as if even the singing insects in the darkening garden, even the ripples on the surface of the pond, the clicking bamboo leaves and the breeze

that stirred them must be still when the other minister
allowed his magnificence to radiate nearby.

"You know Lady Aoi?" the princess's father said.

"Of course, of course." He was busy radiating and
did not glance at her. Aoi had not met him before. She
murmured greetings and raised her open fan before
her face.

"Misfortune strikes in the oddest places," the other
minister said, without addressing either of them directly. "Your daughter has everything to make her
happy, yet some obscure fault in her karma has
suddenly manifested itself and her house and all her
belongings are gone."

"It is not quite—"

But the other minister went on. "How distressing
for you." And he turned his smile on the minister,
clearly implying that the fault, whether of lack of
prudence or bad karma or offense to the gods, was in
the minister and not in his daughter. "We," he said,
meaning his own illustrious family, "have had no
fires."

He broke off to flick the fan at his sleeve, crushing a
disobedient fold that puffed too high. "Akimitsu told
me. He said you missed meeting him this morning
and then sent him a note. I," he said, "never write my
own notes. Akimitsu does all that for me."

"Yes," said the minister, "it is good fortune that
you have such an able secretary."

"One needs useful men when one has the responsibility of government. Akimitsu," he sniffed, and he
was a man who knew how to sniff a person's name
into insignificance, "is perhaps a little too much the
servant, but he is always there at my elbow at the
council meetings, always hands me the needed docu-
ment, says into my ear what each man means to ask—
they speak in circles, you know," he said to Aoi,
"never plainly. But one can tangle oneself in politenesses for hours and never get to the tassel at the end
of the cord, so to speak. Akimitsu doesn't hear all the

sweetness of the fleshing out, he goes right to the bone. Useful, I think that is really the very best word. He is useful and he works hard. Up late at night, then rises before dawn for his meeting with you." Briefly he faced the minister, whose expression of interest and encouragement seemed to make him uneasy, so that he shifted his gaze to the garden. "I worry about Akimitsu sometimes, he looks so—well, his eyes quite swim in redness when he has been working late. I try to make him take a nap but he won't." He turned again to Aoi. "I know that sleeping in the daytime is improper but one must be practical and I never hesitate myself, if my duties have kept me late at the banquet table." He moved a little on his cushion, so that he could lean closer to Aoi, to favor her with further secrets of the art of government. "He does all my edicts. Without such skilled help, you know, I would not be able . . . I am a man who is very deliberate. I must relax and think carefully, I cannot be pushed. But once I decide, then I rest. After one has turned a matter over carefully—Ah, well, I should not give away my methods. But with this man's help I rule with confidence. A word to Akimitsu and a thing is done."

The princess's father had listened with a bemused expression. His comment of "Really?" into the slight pause in the other minister's monologue had no edge to it. The other minister turned confidentially to him.

"Akimitsu will not rise—a pity. But he has not that knowledge of place. Oh, I know he is son of an emperor—a long-ago emperor and perhaps a not very important one, but we must give him his due. I hear that he has built himself a little house—that is very nice for him, that monstrous old place of his grandmother's surely requires a lot of keeping up. But Akimitsu does not—Well, he does not quite stand up as a man."

He looked firmly and sorrowfully at the minister, who said, "I see."

"He whispers and hints, he slides around at the

back of the room. He bows to everyone too much, he holds nothing back. A man must save some respect for himself. And yet, once he feels he knows you, he can be quite arrogant."

"I understand you perfectly," said the minister, making certain small deliberate movements toward rising that caused the other minister to decide, with a look of worried confusion, that his visit was over.

"We do not often meet these days. It is pleasant to have this chance . . . Lady . . . ?" He had already forgotten her name. She returned his bow, and, keeping her head lowered, she could hear that the minister accompanied him to the outer gate, speaking pleasantly and with sincere cordiality the whole way.

Left alone, Aoi was reminded by the coming darkness that she should by now be walking the white paths that lead to the inner recesses of the palace grounds. She thought of how the emperor would wait for her, his eyes burning and watering, and she wondered if someone had told him of the fire at the princess's house, so that he might understand why she did not come. She was not in her usual residence and had no man to send with a message. And the minister, who had meant to make the explanation himself, had now been delayed. All the day's fright, upset, dislocation, and frustration overcame her. When the minister returned she was unable to speak as she bowed and made movements to leave. He understood at once.

"Since I have not been at court today, there is still one more person I must meet. He is just arriving but I came ahead to reassure you. I have sent a messenger to His Majesty and as soon as—"

An angry voice cut in as a monk appeared in the doorway. He dropped to his knees with a clatter of bones, bowed briefly, and sat up. The set of his elbows, too far out at the sides, was an affront to the minister, as was the hectoring and impatient voice. "When there is only one official one must see, and when that official is not to be found . . . Forgive me, but how can a government keep running when its key

man makes himself unavailable? I am surprised to
find you so lax in your duty. If even you . . . Ah,
standards decline, there is self-indulgence everywhere."

"You have not heard that my daughter's house was
set on fire this morning and that she and her ladies
barely escaped?"

Aoi had hidden her face as soon as she saw the
man's religious habit and he, aware that a woman sat
in the twilight of the room, kept his head turned so as
not to see her. He was thin and pale, a man still young
but pinched in the face, his eyes intense, deep lines set
between them. He spoke as if hurling his words
forward on a stream of force that he allowed to escape
and then cut and confined with tight lips. Aoi had
heard him preach. It was Genson, the diviner.

"Such misfortunes do not strike the virtuous," the
monk said and the minister regarded him quizzically.
"You may give me an offering and I will order
prayers."

"You would have me offer gold when so much is
lost?"

"Honor the Buddha most of all at times of loss and
thus teach yourself spiritual values. Gold is but a
thing of the world."

"And yet so popular with this priest," the minister
murmured to Aoi as she began to gather her skirts. To
Genson he said, "Ah, theology, theology."

Aoi moved toward the door and the monk replied,
"But duty is not suspended by small misfortunes."

The minister, knowing the extent of Aoi's exhaustion, touched her elbow as she passed. It was an
almost unseen gesture but enough to connect the
current of sympathy that always ran between them.
Aoi had to pass Genson and the monk scurried
backward, as if to avoid filth. She changed her course
and left by the garden verandah.

Chapter 5

The next day Aoi made a trip to the market. She would buy dye powders for the new clothes the princess wanted to make, and common medicinal herbs. If she looked also for blue vitriol, no one would notice. She asked Lady Miyuki to go with her.

"I don't think you have seen the palace market. Do me a favor and keep me company."

Miyuki flushed and turned away, saying, "I would find nothing to buy."

"Oh but this market has imported marvels, it is where all the Chinese merchants have their stalls."

"I have only this unsuitable robe."

She was wearing one of the robes sent by the wardrobe people. Aoi looked her over. "It is true that gray is a sober color meant for mourning or for an older person. But this subdued cloth on a young woman is pleasing and unexpected. However"—she turned away—"if you don't want to come . . ." and she started off to have O-hana tie up her hair with ribbons to keep it from getting blown about and tangled.

"I will be ready immediately," said Lady Miyuki, her face not quite interested but her steps hastening as she went down the hall.

Though the weather was still warm, the humidity had cleared during the night and the sky was blue with small clouds that drifted rapidly east. They went in the minister's split palmleaf carriage. Lady Miyuki sat facing the front blind, watching the driver, who walked beside the ox waving a long switch and the runner who led the way. She did not seem interested in the scene around them, as they passed into a main avenue. Aoi looked the opposite way, through the blind over the rear gate, seeing the runner who followed them, wearing the minister's livery, and the many other carriages passing in both directions. Among these threaded foot traffic of laborers, peddlers, messengers, women with tied-up bundles, children, dogs, and occasionally leashed monkeys. Aoi heard a small exclamation from her companion and turned. One of the monkeys had jumped onto the ox's back, causing it to leap aside. The carrriage swayed, the driver flicked his switch, the child jerked the monkey down and ran to his mother. But the driver laughed and motioned that the monkey could ride for a while. So the carriage of the Great Minister of the Right arrived at the palace market with a monkey squatted on the haunches of its ox, a capering boy alongside, a bowing woman plucking at his sleeve, and a driver pretending that all was normal. People smiled.

Lady Miyuki looked back at Aoi in surprise. "Won't the minister be angry?"

"No."

It was midmorning and the market section was busy. Aoi asked the runners to stop some distance away, not wanting to displace lesser carriages, as a minister's carriage could do. The ox was unyoked and led to the tethering field, the traces were tipped slightly downward, a stool was placed between them, and the ladies dismounted. The runners walked behind them as they moved into the crowd.

Aoi soon found that Lady Miyuki was not so much interested in shopping as in being seen with the minister's men. She paced and stopped, posing herself as if looking into a stall, but seeing not exotic silks and jewelry but the instant respect of the sellers. Aoi was impatient to look for garlic, castor seeds, green laver, star grass roots, beeswax, and other supplies that were not particularly exotic. Signaling to one of the runners to stay with Lady Miyuki, she took the other one with her, moving quickly to the herb sellers, where she crumbled pinches of dried leaves, smelled for freshness, carried them into the sunlight to check their color, bought powders, roots, barks, pods, and leaf teas.

At every place she asked for old Kamo, the maker of medicines. No one knew anything about him, where he lived or if he lived. She had trouble finding the stall of Li, the man from Silla who sold the best ginseng. Finally after searching the area where she thought she remembered he had had his stall for some years, she was told by a broad woman who spoke loudly because of her own deafness that Li had been closed up the day before and sent to Kyushu to find a ship that would take him home.

"You mean he has been deported?"

"Yes, left, left."

"But was he forced to go? And why?"

The woman, not hearing clearly, smiled and repeated that the man had left, that this had been his stall and it was given now to her by the market authorities. Li had been a friend of Kamo, and Aoi had thought that certainly he would have been able to tell her where to find him.

When finally she had bought all the items on her mental list, she went looking for Lady Miyuki and found her in a jade shop, which she had actually entered. She was standing near the blind that formed the side wall of the merchant's tiny space and she held in her hand a small white figure of a sheep reclining on folded legs. The almost translucent pure white of the jade seemed to fascinate her.

"Look," she said as Aoi joined her.

Lady Miyuki held the carving in her palm, feeling the weight of it, folding her fingers to stroke its smoothness. "It's warm," she said wonderingly.

"Warm," said a voice, "and luminous. Like your skin, like your full cheek."

Aoi looked up. A man had spoken from the shop on the other side of the blind. But as she tried to see who it was, Aoi was struck by the effect of the filtered sunlight on Lady Miyuki's appearance. She stood in rays of sun and shadow from the blind, her hair and her profile glowing all the more for the spacing of the light. Through the blind they could see a man in fine clothes. Lady Miyuki's fan was instantly drawn from her belt and opened to cover all but her eyes. She looked down and was perfectly still, the white carving cupped in her hand.

"My heart is stopped to see you there. You are a figure from my dreams," the man said, his voice low.

Lady Miyuki began to tremble. She leaned toward Aoi as if she might fall. Aoi made a sign to the runners, took the carving and handed it back to the shop man, pressed Lady Miyuki's elbow, and began to draw her away.

"But who are you?" came from beyond the blind. And then, "Ah." He must have seen the runners in livery he recognized.

That ended their shopping. On the way home Aoi was disturbed by the change in Miyuki. She was now neither pretending to be bored nor lively and interested. Her color was mottled as if circulation had stopped, she hunched her shoulders and hugged her arms across her body, clearly suffering. The incident had been unusual but not offensive and Aoi could not understand this reaction. It will be something to tell the princess, she thought. And if the man does indeed trace her to the minister's house, it will become a matter of interest for us all. The princess would welcome an element of romance among her ladies.

Within an hour and before Aoi had mentioned the encounter, a messenger boy came to the main gate with a package "for the lady of the jade shop." The princess did not understand who was meant by this name and Aoi explained. Lady Miyuki was not with them. She had gone to her room, saying she felt sick from the hot morning sun. Aoi would have liked to let Lady Miyuki tell the story herself, or at least to have her present so that there was no feeling of talking behind her back. But it was impossible to turn away the questions the princess asked and Aoi told her of the words a man had spoken from behind a shop blind.

"Did you get a look at him?" asked the princess.

"I could see that he was well-dressed."

"And he spoke to . . . Lady Miyuki?" This was Lady Takumi, to whom such an adventure would have seemed only what was to be expected. She kept her face carefully blank, lest the princess scold her for unkindness, but her inflection was of unbelief.

"At just that moment Lady Miyuki was quite beautiful," Aoi said.

"And this package, this will be the jade animal, don't you think?" said Lady Omi.

"Oh, yes," said the princess, and again, "Oh, yes." She took the package and turned it delicately with the ends of her fingers. It was wrapped in green brocade and tied with a white satin cord. Aoi saw that the princess lightly stroked the cloth as she set the box down. She saw also that she forced away romantic thoughts. "Probably some philanderer of the guards," and the princess tried to put scorn into her voice.

"Shall I call her?" Lady Omi went to rouse the lady of the jade shop.

Resting had calmed Lady Miyuki and she took up the box with her usual detached air. "Need I open it now?"

"We will never forgive you if you don't," said the princess.

Under the green silk was a second wrapping of soft white paper and narrow green ribbon intricately tied. When the knot had been undone with much trouble not to damage the ribbon, the paper fell away from a pale wooden box. Inside was a further nesting of white satin and green paper that unfolded to reveal the little carving. A note on a square of gray writing paper, which was what they had all been looking for, was fitted against one side of the interior of the box.

Lady Miyuki would perhaps have saved this note to read when she was alone, but the eagerness of the princess made that impossible. She unfolded the gray paper, glanced at the writing, and let the note drop. Aoi saw that she was without color or expression as she had been in the carriage on the way home. The princess picked up the paper and read the poem aloud.

> *"What forgotten dream*
> *Of radiance was given*
> *Back to me this day—*
> *You are as gold that was lost*
> *But now gleams from among dust."*

"Not a very subtle poem," said Lady Takumi.

"But rather a nice image, don't you think?" said Lady Omi.

"It is quite apt that he speaks of radiance," said Aoi, but she cut short her comment because of the pain in Miyuki's eyes.

The princess, whose opinion would have the most weight and who would indicate if she thought her lady should encourage the man, considered the note as the others talked and watched her carefully. Finally she seemed ready to speak, and they were silent. "Such fine handwriting," she said. "There is nothing obvious about that, it does not faint away with emotion but is free and balanced. I think he is a man who trusts his feelings because he does not waste them. He is probably a person worth knowing."

That decided the question of whether there should be a reply, and only Aoi and Miyuki herself did not join in suggesting return poems. Finally Miyuki said with awkward loudness and force, "I have no desire to see this man alone. If he is to visit, let him visit us all together. And so we will send him a joint reply."

The princess was offended and she turned away saying, "Do as you like." Lady Takumi also, now that Miyuki had blundered, lost interest. Lady Omi was distressed and consoling. "How busily we help you and I am sure you know already what you would like to answer."

Aoi said, "Come. Let's see what paper we can find in my writing box. That will be my part in this, to give you paper. Then we will leave you in peace to write or not as you please."

When they were in her room, Aoi sent O-hana away so that she was alone with Lady Miyuki. She took from her writing box a packet of many kinds of paper.

"You can see," she said, displaying a variety of colors and textures, "that paper is one of my weaknesses. Beauty and usefulness, both irresistible qualities, are combined in paper, and I collect it with really deplorable energy. But"—she put down the spread handful of crisp sheets—"I can see that you don't want to write a reply to this man's poem."

Miyuki turned her head away and did not speak.

"It is a usual politeness that one answers such a note but it is not required," Aoi said.

Miyuki was still silent. Just when Aoi was wondering if she was crying, she spoke in a cold voice. "Don't bother choosing paper. I will not answer his note. Even so, I think that he will come. But, lady, your room is next to mine. May I ask you . . ."

"I don't like to interfere."

"But if I ask you?"

"Do you feel that you need protection?"

"Not exactly."

"Are you afraid of him—of this one man, of any man?"

"I think perhaps you could say that. But you will know when he comes to me—we never can help hearing what goes on in the adjoining room. Will you sit close to the gallery?"

"And listen?"

"And make some sound if he abuses me. He will not like for another person—"

"You must have had some bad experience in the past, to be so cautious and distrustful."

Lady Miyuki was quiet for a time and when she spoke again it was in a faint, low voice. "Do you know what it is like to turn to stone? To thicken with cold and become heavy, dense, broad, and deeply set? I have almost wakened now and he has come again."

"But you have not yet met him."

"I know him."

Aoi sat thinking. This girl had some strange ideas. She seemed to equate all men with the one who had damaged her trust in the past. Part of the time Aoi could not understand what she was talking about, but Lady Miyuki's emotion was strong, and she always respected strong feeling.

"You are not required to answer the note or to allow the man near you. Pay no attention to the princess, you need not do as she would like."

"Perhaps I want him to come, it is hard to tell."

"But if you are afraid?"

"I will not lose this chance, it may be different this time. Please be my friend."

"I can't promise to listen to your private conversation, even if asked. That is not my nature. But I will put my cushion near the wall and if it happens that I overhear, I suppose I will not trouble to move away."

Miyuki thanked her and left for the adjoining room with a queer expression of satisfaction on her face.

Chapter 6

The minister returned home that evening in a disturbed state. He sat with them and heard the tale of Lady Miyuki's admirer, but Aoi knew him well enough to tell that he was preoccupied and not fully present with them. It had always been a special characteristic of the minister that, with all his duties and involvements in the government and at court, he spoke to every person simply and directly, as if he had nothing on his mind but the moment's talk.

The evenings were closing earlier as the Tenth Month began. Aoi walked into the garden just before dark. All color was intense and the water of the pond was still, reflecting the sky and becoming a new source of light. She sat on a broad stone at the water's edge and after a few minutes heard steps on the path behind her. The minister, as he had always liked to do, had come to speak privately with Aoi.

"I have no desire to prolong this day," he said, "but its end belies its beginning."

"Something is wrong."

"Unh." The minister made an impatient movement of his hand as he sat on the adjoining stone. "An unpleasantness." He was still for long minutes before he explained. Insects sang, a flock of birds crossed the air high up. Aoi waited. "You know my office, how there is space under the building at one end because it is set on a slope."

"Yes."

"This morning a body was found there, just under the building near the steps."

"Such a thing! And in the palace grounds!"

"Hunh. The palace is no better guarded than any other place in this city. We are all cowed." He sat in silence again. "We are cowed by the violence that comes from the western wards and by the priests from the mountains who invade us with arms whenever they are displeased. We don't know how to counter them, we have lost our skills in that way. Only the warlike men of the provinces, whose lack of culture we scorn so . . ."

The timidity of the guards and of the police was well-known. There had been a long spell of trouble with the priests during the spring and, because the armed men of the city had been sent running by the brawling physicality of blows and fists and shouts, the minister and the council had asked for help from a strong landholder in an eastern province. His soldiers had been quartered in one of the several unused buildings within the palace walls and they had done so much damage that the building had been torn down after they left. But they had pursued the priests to the temple estates in the hills, trampling fields and burning buildings, and until recently the priests had not come down again. In the city, crime had increased and thieves had grown bolder. People were stoic, saying that it was the Latter Day of the Law and morals were corroded everywhere.

"And the body?" Aoi said.

"It was a young girl. They had dressed her in gaudy clothes of cheap stiff material. She was much too young for those clothes of gold and red."

"How did she die?"

"There was no wound, we could not tell."

"Who was she?"

"That also we don't know."

"But why . . .?"

"Why? Yes. Why under my office? Because some-one meant to imply a bad thing. This was found in her clothes." He pulled from his belt a fold of rough paper, larger than the usual note, and passed it to her.

It was a crudely drawn ink painting of a fish, the mouth open and toothed, the eye leering, a male appendage drawn just below the tailfin. Blue color was washed over the scales. Aoi glanced at it and folded the paper again.

"You know that poem the emperor made?" the minister said. "I have many times wished he hadn't, though he meant to honor me."

Aoi quoted,

> *"How invisibly*
> *The great fish in the blue deep*
> *Turns in the shadows,*
> *Moving the waters aside,*
> *Creating his own current."*

The emperor had published the poem on the anni-versary of the minister's first year in office, after it had become apparent that he and not the Minister of the Left would be the able man everyone would depend on. The image of a fish in blue water had immediately been changed in the popular mind to that of a blue fish. Now any reference to fish or even to blue was likely to refer to the Great Minister of the Right, so powerful but so discreet. The implication of the finding of the drawing would be clear to anyone: that the minister had sent for a very young girl, used her for pleasure, and left her dead.

"Surely no one believes . . . Do people know?"

"Oh, yes. The guards made a great fuss. This was something that did not endanger them and they were busy, loud, and officious."

Aoi could think of no comfort to offer. They were both quiet for a long time. "This thing, I do not like it," he said at last. "The finding of a dead body, that is not so unusual. But the fish picture . . ." He paused and looked out over the patterned water. "It means that someone moves against me. And more seriously than the usual jealousy and lies. It seems to me somehow womanly in its slyness. But"—he laughed—"I don't have much to do with women. What do *you* think?"

"There are times, certainly, when women ambitious for their sons or eager to place daughters at court have slandered very successfully. But the placing of a body . . . I think that, even if she were to use an agent, a plot with so much of a physical element would be beyond any woman who might be high enough to profit if you were harmed. What person, though, would benefit from blighting your reputation?"

"I suppose the other minister comes most readily to mind. But I feel that he is content with the glory of his office, and I know he is too lazy to seek more work."

"Who would take your place if—forgive me—you should be . . ." Aoi could not say aloud the word *exiled.* No man of the court could bear the idea of removal from the world above the clouds, as it was called, where the emperor and those around him existed. Only in that world was life refined to a perfection of physical surroundings, dress, social nicety, and art, only in that world were influence and serious government position possible. Provincial governors might go away for a few years to enrich themselves with the taxes that passed through their hands, but however grand their local status, they never failed to lament their absence from the capital. Men of that world might retire into religion when they grew older, but they often kept much of their influence and income. Forced departure into exile, whether gently done or resulting in death from mistreatment during the journey, was the ultimate punishment.

"Ah well," the minister said. "Perhaps we shall find interest in all this, you and I, with our analyzing instincts. Will a little mystery exercise our brains?"

"Something nicer, please, the evening is too sweet to concern ourselves with nasty pictures and dead bodies. The problem of a poem will do for my exercise.

> *"Living in water,*
> *The great fish of the blue deep*
> *Simply floats above . . ."*

She left the poem unfinshed and he made the last two lines.

> *"Mud clouds stirred from the bottom.*
> *But do they hide the fishnet?"*

He turned his head toward her. "How is it that we have spent so much time apart?" he said. "No other person has your sympathy and good sense."

They sat together until it was dark and a chill wind blew in over the walls. The soft warmth of this unseasonable autumn was nearly gone.

Chapter 7

My messenger has
Strong legs, my heart is as strong.
But pity for us—
Poor legs, poor heart—would let me
Come to speak my love direct.

This man complains of the distance between
us that he must travel so many times a day.
If I could make the trip only once!

It was late afternoon, almost dark, and the day was
cloudy. The note was the fifth one that day and it was
written on gray paper as all the others had been. Lady
Miyuki received it reluctantly, unfolding it delicately
as if she would like not to touch it and letting it drift
from her hand for the others to see. She had become
watchful and quiet, she moved about her duties with
many small glances at Aoi, self-conscious and uncertain. Lady Takumi's mood was sour. Lady Omi sym-
pathized with everyone—with the man in his ardor,
with Lady Miyuki in her indecision, Aoi in her

cautious detachment, and the princess in her eagerness to see love met with love. She did not approach
Lady Takumi because she disapproved of envy.

The minister had left early, before the ladies waked,
and they had not seen him. Aoi had sent O-hana into
the city with an unliveried man to accompany her.
She was to search for Kamo the medicine maker or
any other person who might have the blue crystals. In
midafternoon the prince had come again to see his
wife, riding in with only one man, passing through the
halls as naturally as if he were in his own home,
coughing politely outside the princess's door. To Aoi's
surprise, the princess, influenced perhaps by her father's tolerance, admitted him as if there had been no
previous refusal. The ladies left them alone and they
talked for a long time. In the evening he was still
there.

The day had been warm. Just at dark a light rain
began to fall, stopping and starting again, making
pleasant splashing sounds on the leaves and stones of
the garden.

In this large house all the ladies had private rooms.
Aoi sat late with a light beside her writing table. She
was trying to compose a hopeful letter for the emper-
or, without telling him she had been unable to find
more medicine for his eyes. She was worried. It was
said that, before she began the treatment that had
given him so much hope, he had talked of retiring in
favor of his son, who was only sixteen and, if one were
to acknowledge the truth, a little dim. What would
happen if the medicine could not be replaced?

The house was quiet. Lady Takumi, bored and
petulant because of the attention paid to Lady Miyuki
today, was probably sitting just behind her blind with
a wide spread of skirts allowed to spill underneath,
hoping that a friend would think to call on her this
soft night. Lady Omi, Aoi thought, sat the same way,
but farther into her room so that she could not be
seen, even as a shadow, from outside. Rainy weather

always made her sad and she would think of her dead husband and of her three children, who lived with his mother and father. She was lonely for them but she recognized her good fortune in having duties, lots of company, and a good income. The princess would be enjoying the unusual intimacy with her husband. The minister had not yet returned home.

Lady Miyuki, beyond the connecting wall, would surely have put her cushion behind a curtain screen. Aoi could hear that she folded and unfolded the gray-paper notes, reciting the poems to herself in the dark. There was a rustle of robes on the verandah.

"Is it our fate always to have bamboo between us?" It was the same voice they had heard in the jade shop. As she had promised Miyuki, Aoi did not move away.

"I knew," Miyuki said, "that you would persuade the servants to let you in. Servants always think that lovers are harmless."

"What an unwelcoming thing to say, especially since you do not know me at all."

"Don't I?" Miyuki's voice became indistinct, as if she had turned her head in another direction. "You will have your way, do what you want, enter where you will. You are a prince and you expect that to excuse anything."

"Hunh. It is wet out here. Will you have me ruin my clothes?" The blind struck the doorframe as he moved it aside, footsteps advanced into Miyuki's room.

"I have only to cry out . . ." Lady Miyuki could not speak quite calmly, her voice was higher-pitched than usual, and it seemed that she could not breathe well.

"You puzzle me," he said. "I saw you in an extraordinary moment and I have truly fallen in love. I don't know what it is about you. It is as if rightness suddenly blessed my life. I feel redeemed to have found you. It hurts me to hear you speak with such hostility, when finally we sit in the same room. And how can you tell that I am a prince?"

"Perhaps we have known each other in a previous life."

"How bitterly you say that. I mean only to please you. Won't you let me come a little nearer?"

"It can't be helped," Miyuki said, speaking to herself. "I would look a fool if I made a fuss. There is really nothing I can do." She was not quite tearful, though she seemed to be urging herself to cry.

"You sound very sad and that is certainly unflattering. I am not a man to be ashamed of. And surely you understand my passion, surely you cannot think I will come here once or twice and then abandon you." There were brushing sounds and Aoi thought that he moved forward little by little. "I mean to have you—"

"—for you own. Yes, I know."

"It was like a heavenly being had come to stand beside me, there in the jade shop, arrayed in light."

"Don't call me a heavenly being. I am not even fully alive as a human being. I am not a good person."

"But you must understand my need of you."

"Ah, need. One takes what one needs. Why don't you speak of giving?"

"One can be given what one needs—for love."

"When I was in love—it was long ago—I wanted to be generous. I was beautiful then, too young to have turned against myself. All my love was open, I trusted that what I gave would come back to me. But he, that man I loved—" For a moment she could not control her voice. "My fresh body, my wish to give him ease, my joy when he was with me, my faith and loyalty— he took all these gifts but gave me criticism and demand, neglect and physical coldness, abuse, and eventually total absence. Do you think that you have never been like that?"

"Please don't compare me to that kind of man."

"But you begin as he did, with your own need and talk of taking."

"What can I give you, if life in a fine new house,

with a man of high standing, provided with every comfort, served night and day by discreet women, does not seem to you a gift?"

"And will you be with me, in this fine house?"

"Of course, it is where I live." His voice became tight and deep. "It is a man's way to take what he wants. I am no weak poem maker of the capital. I was raised to master horses and cheating farmers. These sweet nice feelings you speak of are not in me, I am better without them. And if I am attracted to you, it may be because you too are better for what happened long ago. You have put away pretense. Cruel as it seems to me, you speak your mind. And I am more than ever in love with you, more than ever determined—"

"My arm," she said. "You are hurting me."

"Cruel, cruel." There was ecstasy in his voice. "You cannot be first wife, it is true. My principal wife—"

"Very highborn."

"Actually, yes, a relation of the royal family. What a curious person you are, with your intuition. But she lives in a separate place, you would be mistress in your own mansion." His voice descended again to deep angry tones. "Be a little kinder."

Miyuki began to cry, her breath uneven, as if he shook her.

"It is unbearable," he said, "to be received like this. Must I leave, without seeing again the beauty that . . ."

The curtain he had raised fell back into place with a swish of silk, heels struck the floor as he stood up.

"When I come next, I will ask if I may see you. Only if you consent will I be here. No more persuasion by note. I must speak my case in person. Sleep well."

A rattle of blind, a few footfalls on the outside boards, and he was gone. Lady Miyuki continued to cry, drawing many shaking breaths, as if she could not fill her lungs. Aoi waited but Miyuki did not speak to her from beyond the wall and she went to bed.

In the morning as the prince was dressing to leave,

the subject of Lady Miyuki's lover came up when Lady Takumi said that her maid had told her of Miyuki's visitor. The princess, who had been so avidly interested, did not want to draw unfavorable comparisons just at this time and she did not say much about it. But Lady Takumi made an amusing story of the many notes and the exhaustion of the busy messenger, with teasing glances at Miyuki that were not entirely kind.

"He has even sent a note to my lady, to ask her to use her influence," she said, teasing again in revealing to the prince that his wife had accepted a note from an unknown man.

"Yes, a very forward person, whoever he is." The princess was uneasy but she took the note from her writing box, as if she feared not to show it immediately.

"But I know that handwriting," said the prince. "How many times I have seen it on official documents! Your mysterious lover is Akimitsu, who serves as secretary to the other minister. I am surprised. You must have made a strong impression on him, Lady Miyuki. He is always very interested in his duties."

They all turned to Miyuki but she was moving toward a shelf in the back of the room where toilet supplies were stored and she did not let them see her face.

"If you have any mercy in you," the princess said to her husband, "tell us more about him. Even Lady Takumi doesn't know him, and I know that Miyuki will be interested."

Miyuki had come back with an incense burner in her hand, stiff-faced.

"He is a sort of forgotten son of the old emperor, only child of a favorite concubine, I think. There are strange stories. That he was the pet of his grandmother and unmanageable as a child. That when she died, he was taken to the provinces and grew up there. That his income—" The prince suddenly looked blank. "The story is that his estates were annexed by your father but that is, of course, untrue. People will say anything about those who have risen high."

"What happened to his mother?" asked Lady Omi.

"Her mind was not strong. Or her health, I don't know the truth of it. But her trouble was that there was no family influence to back her. The emperor was extremely fond of her, and the other court women were so jealous that they persecuted her until she left. Even His Majesty could not bring her back, they say. After they took her child from her, she died of grief."

"This about my father," the princess said, "is preposterous. It is much more likely that he kept the man's estates intact and even used his influence to place him with the other minister."

"Of course. I should not have repeated what jealous people say. But this story has been very strong lately and, low or high, everyone seems to believe it."

Aoi was remembering an incident from long ago but she did not speak. It seemed important to find out what kind of man that strange child had become.

"Is he handsome?" This was the first question Lady Takumi had asked.

The prince seemed unable to decide on his answer. "He is tall," he said at last. "He has a kind of elegance. He knows surprising things, because of his provincial background. He occasionally makes mistakes with the gentlemen of the council, misjudges, offends them."

Aoi thought that Akimitsu must be a man who made more than a surface impression, since the prince's description had moved from appearance to character.

Lady Miyuki was perfuming the prince's outer robe, moving the smoking censer up and down inside it. The others suddenly turned to her, avid for reaction, spiteful, or apologetic for embarrassing her, according to their several natures. But Miyuki clung to the protection of her normal indifference and continued the slow movements of her arm.

Just then a maid came saying that there was another

letter for the lady of the jade shop. She spoke the name with coy smiles, one with the others in a romantic plot. Miyuki set down the censer and held the robe for the prince to put on. The maid had left the note on the floor where the princess sat and it was not until the prince had settled all his collars and belts that Miyuki took it up.

She opened it, then let it drop. The princess spread the paper open with her fingertips, showing them all that the paper was blank. Miyuki, finally affected by the concentrated attention of the others, pulled her sleeve across her face and left the room. Aoi had seen that her expression was peculiarly grim, though she smiled.

Chapter 8

As the prince was leaving, Aoi walked with him along the corridor. "The emperor asks for you. He is very troubled with his eyes and he doesn't understand why you don't come," he said.

"We have sent messages and I thought that the minister would speak to him. I have written him myself that my medicines were stolen. Surely after all this he understands the reason."

"I don't know, there are strange people around him these days, doctors, diviners, mystic priests. They are likely to intercept people and messages. Can't you get more of the medicine?"

Aoi explained about the old pharmicist and how she had looked for him. The prince stopped walking and turned to her. "Do you know of the man they call the Combmaker?"

"That strange beggar person? I have heard you speak of him."

"There is not a place in the city he doesn't know, east or west. I sometimes ask his help. He is good at tracing those who disappear or hide and he always knows"—he laughed—"more than he should. I will send out word and we will see if he can be found."

A message came later in the day. The prince had a house in a modest district and Aoi was to meet him there. The princess did not know of this house and Aoi deceived her about her errand. But the minister's carriage man did not seem surprised when she gave him directions. Aoi recognized, as she had before, that the presumed privacy of the aristocracy was an illusion.

A midddle-aged woman seemed to be the one servant in the house. She led Aoi to sit behind a curtain in a clean and rather bare room that opened onto a garden with a stone-lined pool and water lilies. The prince arrived soon after. The woman served them wine and peeled pears.

"I must tell you that this man will play the fool and it is much better if he doesn't see you. Make an opening," he separated the curtain from the frame at one end, "he will sit here," he touched the floor at some distance in front of him, "and you will be able to see him."

They waited. The woman came to say that the man they expected had sent word that he would be late. She brought cold noodles. They waited. It was hot. Insects whirred in the garden. Gold carp circled the lilies in the pond. The woman came to say that he was here but she thought she shouldn't let him in. She mumbled in embarrassment and they caught the word *drunk*.

The prince smiled. "You think he is drunk? Bring him here and we shall see."

Aoi leaned closer to the curtain, to put the door in her line of vision. The man came in on his knees, bowing very properly.

"For a long time you have neglected me," he said, turning the customary polite greeting upside down. "I am happy to—" A violent hiccup interrupted his speech and he collapsed from the recoil of it, falling almost flat in a clatter of knocking elbows and knuckles. "Oopsh." His nose seemed stuck to the floor, his arms without strength or coordination to raise him. His clothes of layers of soft rags were fluid around him, spreading and lifting as he moved. When finally he had both elbows high at the same time and both palms on the floor, he pushed himself upright, but overdid it and fell at once to the side nearest Aoi, catching himself on a stiff arm and aiming his good eye—the other one looked off at an angle—at the space between the curtain and the frame. Jerking up in surprise, he pushed air between his teeth. "Ish," he said to the prince, "thersh a lady," and with severity, "Ith there alwayth a lady in thith houthe? I don't remember thith one, but she'th thertainly . . ." and he brought his wayward eye in line, smiled with modest sweetness, dropped into another bow, and finished in modulated perfect diction, "due more respect than I have shown her," and turning to bow again, "Please favor me, Lady Aoi, and forgive my joke." When he sat up only wit and intelligence lit his face.

The prince was laughing. "How do you know who this lady is?" he said.

"An eye that is open tends to see."

"We have need of your eyes just now. The lady seeks a medicine seller—"

"—named Kamo. Is that all?"

"You know him then?"

"I don't know him, I only know that Lady Aoi looks for him. But priests are my meat."

The prince explained to Aoi. "He hates priests. It was because of priests that this man lost his family. He used to have a small house and workshop near the Eastern Market and lived there with his wife and little daughter. He made fine boxwood combs for the Office of the Empress's Household. But his house was overrun in a fight between priests of Kiyomizu Temple and Todai Temple and both the wife and child died of injuries when a wall fell on them."

"I have been in a rage ever since," said the Combmaker with a sweet smile.

"I remember those combs," said Aoi, "and I have one still, with a design of pine needles. Do you make them now?"

The Combmaker's eye slid to its off-looking angle, his smile loosened again to drunkenness, he spoke with thick tongue. "Ish. Howsh to make combsh now? And why?" The intensity of this question straightened his features and his speech and he said again, "Why?" He let his chin fall onto his chest and they were all quiet.

"I have great and urgent need of the medicine seller," Aoi said at last. She told him where the man Kamo had lived before and all she knew of him.

"Well, we will see what we can do."

"He calls in many to help, people of the streets," the prince said.

"Yes, yes." The Combmaker seemed to think this request a minor one. "The priests do not worry you?" he said to the prince.

"In what way?"

"They are busy, they meet, they come and go." He paused. "Do you know that diviner person who casts bones?"

"Genson."

"Yes, that one. Genson is very popluar these days."

"I don't understand you." But the Combmaker had put on his drunkenness, as if he had dissolved and slipped away, becoming a blurred and coarsened figure who took awkward leave and flopped a few bows, rising and subsiding out the door.

"A touching man," Aoi said, moving aside the screen.

"Unh. Sometimes he really is drunk and then he is hopeless. At times he disappears. That is his great talent—not to be seen. He is the kind of invisible person who is not noticed, and so he can pick up all sorts of secrets. The priests especially, he is fond of saying, do not see such a pitiful wretch."

"It is almost frightening, the way he reduces himself. I imagine he takes the blame in some way for the loss of his family, and that is why he . . ."

The prince looked surprised, then uninterested. "Actually he calls himself idiot for caring so much for his family and for making combs. He says that anyone but an idiot knows not to put so much trust in the things of this world. But he blames the priests for what happened and not himself. Come." He stood up and called to the servant and to the man he had left waiting in the courtyard. "I will go back with you. I must see my father-in-law."

Chapter 9

They waited until late in the night for the minister to return, sitting in the main hall with no blind between them and the garden. It was hot and still, clouds covered the moon and stars. Lady Takumi had caught fireflies in a gauze cage. Their light was concentrated enough to make reflections on the floor near the edge of the verandah where the cage had been set. Lady Omi had tuned her koto and she was playing "Here Where the Reeds Sway." She struck the broken chords slowly because she was not expert, but that only made the music pensive. The princess and the prince sat side by side. Lady Miyuki was weeping so quietly that no one but Aoi, who was next to her, could hear. Wondering what on earth could have so moved this leaden lady, Aoi reached out to touch her sleeve but drew back her hand as Miyuki straightened and turned her head from side to side, shaking off her tears.

The minister spoke from behind them. They had not heard the servants run when he arrived, did not know how long he had stood there ungreeted, watch-

ing this peaceful and well-populated scene in his
house that was usually empty of family.

> *"There are some moments*
> *The mirror never forgets."*

He quoted from an old poem. They all stirred at
once but he sat down quickly beside the prince and
they were still again. The minister loosened his belts
and removed his top robe, handing it to a maid, along
with his court fan, the ivory wand that signified his
office, and a few small cases containing personal
articles, saying "Ah" as he lightened himself and "Ah,
how quiet" as he looked from one to the other.

Lady Omi renewed her playing. They listened without speaking, langorous with the hot weather and the
late hour. A maid came, all smiles behind her bobbing
short hair, and motioned that she had a message for
Miyuki. There were whispers and Miyuki went into
the house and did not return. Still they sat. The only
light came from the nervous glow of the fireflies in
Lady Takumi's gauze box.

> *"Light now here now there—*
> *No constancy in a cage*
> *Of fireflies, no shine*
> *Of steady glow to count on,*
> *Even in the blackest dark."*

The minister spoke the poem in a low voice. Lady
Takumi understood the reference to her cage as
attention to herself and laughed with delight, beginning an answering poem. Lady Omi, seeing that
Takumi would break the mood of the evening,
stopped her with a hand on her arm and soon took her
off to bed, a naughty child who did not know what she
had done wrong, flouncing and offended as she gathered up her skirts. She left the fireflies where they
were, only opening the door of the cage so they could
escape when they chose.

After the disturbance of the ladies' departure, the minister put out his hand to detain the others. When he spoke it was to Aoi. "Do you know, lady, the longing to quit the world? These two"—he indicated his daughter and her husband—"are too young for that, but you and I— The peace of solitude in some mountain place, doesn't that tempt us?"

"Very often I think of it," Aoi said.

"What holds us then? What makes us endure . . ."

"Father, you are of a questioning mind tonight."

"Ah yes, I question. Activity of the brain, a curse. Why should this be so and not that? What is that brain thinking and what does it want? Is this word true, is that man false? Is duty a requirement of others or only of my own idea of myself? Unph."

They waited until he should go on.

"They say I take on too much. I try to resign and they say I do it to force them to see that they cannot manage without me. The councillors send excuses, they are ill, every one of them at once. Do it yourself, you are so sure you know best, is what they mean in those notes about head colds and weak livers. The other minister suddenly comes to life, he is issuing edicts all day long. 'The wearing of red and purple has gotten out of hand,' he writes, 'the lowborn are imitating royalty. So-and-so is promoted. People should not talk to foreigners lest they be spies. Special doors should be made for the palace audience hall'— on which the minister himself will do the calligraphy, he who never even writes his own letters! 'Priests of Kofuku Temple are forbidden to act unlawfully. Palace women shall not dress so gaudily. Priests must read in a loud voice, so they can be understood.' And, most important of all, he puts forth his daughter— again—as concubine for the poor emperor."

He turned to Aoi. "The emperor sent for you yesterday."

"Oh?"

"You received no imperial message?"

"No."

"You see. They disobey even the emperor. He could not understand why you didn't come. They probably say that they are protecting him from a woman who wishes him ill, being connected with me."

"Father, surely you exaggerate, no one would slander you so. And if they did, the emperor would never believe . . ."

"What he would believe," said the prince, "is that there are people who want to make trouble for you. I came this evening to warn you of one person." Hearing this, the princess drew away from him. She had thought he came because of her. Aoi expected that he would mention Genson, the "popular" diviner the Combmaker had warned them about. But the prince spoke of another person. "Rumor says you meet that shipbuilding man from Shimosa Province."

"That I meet him? He waylaid me once, in the palace grounds, and wanted to talk. I told him his idea is absurd and I will not support it. I saw him that one time."

"There are those who say that you confer together. They say—forgive me—that there is a plot."

"Ah yes, that is what rumor would say." Usually he would laugh, Aoi thought, at just this kind of wrong-headed interpretation of the most innocent of chance actions. It had always seemed to her that the minister, in his political life, was master player of a game, never allowing himself the spiritual distortions of need and wanting. A little amusement from him just now would reassure her. But his remark held no light tone.

"Who is this man, Father?"

"Taira Munemori. His family are always on the sea and he wants to build a large ship that he says will be very fast. His idea is to carry soldiers as protection against pirates and to trade with China and Silla. But we know his family history of lawlessness. He would become a pirate himself or turn rebel, and with a ship full of armed men, he would attempt to widen his influence. He is a dangerous man and of course I do not meet him."

"I am sorry," said the prince. "I should not trouble you with rumors, perhaps, but . . ."

"Actually you tell me nothing that is new to me. I have not been in office all these years without learning to gather rumors. But I have never before felt that my loyalty was questioned. How can a man know contentment with himself when—" He broke off and turned to Aoi. "Do you hear this, lady? Do you hear how the world has invaded my every thought and word?" And now he laughed. "Am I such an imponderable man that rumor teaches others what I do? Is my character so little apparent that these rumors can be believed? Am I only a minister of this government, a man with a tool of office in his hand, and have no self beyond that position?"

But Aoi could not smile. Official position does not exist without public support, she thought, and even strong identities can be eroded by accusation and attack.

"I know what you are thinking, lady." The minister leaned toward Aoi, his voice was intimate and affectionate in her ear.

She bent her head, acknowledging doubt. "I am not sure that even you can come through this kind of thing."

"Ah but I do not mean to come through." He turned to his daughter and her husband. "I mean to resign. I will not try to justify. If I were to do that, might I not find ambition in myself?"

"The emperor will not accept your resignation. He depends on you, especially now that he is so ill," said the princess.

"I will offer again and again until he is convinced of my sincerity and accepts."

"Actually . . ." The prince pitched his voice low, as if to deny what he was about to say. "Actually you may have to deal with a different emperor."

"Yes, he may abdicate. And then I will have no trouble resigning."

"At this moment, Father, you want to be rid of all

these troubles, so you talk of leaving office. But will you be content to—"

"If I can leave with honor, I will be content, yes—to oversee my gardeners, manage my estates, visit temples, and attend to piety."

Aoi heard in his voice the wish that he might leave in peace and the clear suspicion that his attempts to resign would also be turned against him.

They watched the fireflies in the cage, leaving one by one as they discovered the open door. Their light, in the dark of the garden, seemed lonely and weak, now that they were no longer together.

Chapter 10

In the following days, the minister was either gone from his house for long hours or returned at unexpected times, when he might sit with the ladies for a while but always ended by going into the garden. Sometimes he walked alone, pacing the sanded paths round and round. Sometimes he changed to old clothes and wooden clogs and worked with the gardeners, pruning, transplanting, propping up the spreading limbs of an old pine, cutting the last lilies and standing them in a vase. He liked to row on the garden pond, often sitting in the boat as it drifted, forgetting to move the oars. There were a few days of rain. He got soaked and muddy, came in stomping, happy, sat in the steam of the bath house, and then went out again without a word to anyone.

In fact, after the night when they watched the fireflies escape the gauze cage, he said nothing about his worries at court. Even so, the house became tense around him. The princess kept her ladies sewing and was so silent herself that normal chatter was suppressed. The maids, usually so easy in their manner, so certain of the needs of their master and of their ability to meet them, became by turns slow-pacing and hesitant or, aware that the bows of the guards often thrummed in warning during the nights and sensing trouble, boisterous in their solidarity and determination to defend.

Then there came a morning when news spread from street to street: The emperor had left the palace and moved to a small temple. It was said that he needed rest and prayer in a holy place to heal his eyes. Still the rumor flew that he would abdicate and pass the throne to his son.

The Combmaker came to the kitchen and asked to see Aoi. She received him in a small reception room with no curtain between them. Aoi had decided that the Combmaker, in spite of all his antics, was a man she could trust.

"Well, the priests took him off," he said when he had completed bows and greetings. Today he made no pretense of drunkenness or display of his ability to conceal his true nature. He spoke respectfully, with the rough intonation of porters and vendors that was the natural speech of one born and raised in the city. "So many priests! Here they came, another priest, another priest, move over for one more. So many of them jammed themselves into the carriages of the procession that some of the ladies had to walk. And who do you think has taken charge of the crown prince and visits him at all hours of the day? The other minister. We hear that his daughter is getting together a new wardrobe."

"Yes," said Aoi, "he must expect that if the emperor resigns, he can finally realize his dream of intimate influence in the palace." Aoi felt the wakening stretch of interest. She smiled and said with affection for the amusement his futile posturings and strivings would give her, "The other minister . . ." Because of course the emperor could still be cured, she had only to find more blue vitriol.

The Combmaker, seeming to understand Aoi's line

of thought, laughed for a moment. "But lady," he said, earnest for the first time in her experience of him, "he is not like our minister. We have to watch out for him, bad things could be done with his name on them and he would never know."

"You mean because he is not attentive? Yes, I suppose that carelessness can be dangerous. But tell me, have you found my medicine maker?"

"Yes. Well, that is, no. He died. But he had an apprentice, a man named Kan. We have found him."

Aoi sat up, livened with hope.

"That is," the Combmaker went on, "we have found where he lives but he is not there and his people won't tell us nothing. It seems that suspicious men came looking for him and knocked his brothers around and now he is hiding."

"Suspicious men." It was with a shock of mental engagement that Aoi suddenly saw a pattern of action against the emperor that included herself in the design. The theft of the medicine chest, the removal of the herb man from Silla, and the persecution of old Kamo's apprentice all had the result of preventing her from treating the emperor, and keeping her and her medicine away might lead directly to his abdication. How could she think she would now be allowed near him? Certain people had, perhaps, other desires for the emperor than that he should recover his health and that his mature and intelligent influence should be strong again. Her frivolity of a moment ago in thinking to enjoy the spectacle of the other minister sizzled away like frost on a sunlit leaf. She felt a deep alarm, a sharpening of her faculties, an acuteness of attention, and, most of all, the pleasure of involvement. Ah Aoi, she said to herself. Mountain peace? What emptiness of talk.

"Unh, suspicious men," the Combmaker was continuing. Aoi dragged her attention away from her revealing thoughts. "By the way, lady, did you know that this house was nearly robbed last week?"

"The servants tell us most things." As O-hana had

told her that Akimitsu had spent much of the night before in Lady Miyuki's room.

"They will have told you, then, that there was an argument outside the gate early one morning between two vegetable men on their way to market. But I don't think they know that a man tried to go over the wall while the guards were untangling the cart wheels and quieting the fight."

"You make me uneasy."

"Be glad there was no fire. Same result but tidier—everybody runs to one place while a thief gets into the house somewhere else. Or would have, but my man pulled him down and ran him off."

"Are you guarding us then?"

"We watch, we are good at watching."

He rose to his knees and backed toward the door, bowing and suddenly loose-limbed and lisping. "Thtay well, lady. Even ladieth may need throng conthtituth—conthti— bodieth thethe dayth." He held up a finger as he slid shut the door. "Just practicing."

Chapter 11

"My lady. Forgive me, you must wake up. The minister asks that you come."

"O-hana. What in the world? It must be the middle of the night."

"There is a visitor, he asks that you help receive him."

Aoi, waking so suddenly on a hot night, struggled to draw together her wits and her vision, shielding her eyes from the oil lamp. O-hana handed her a wet cloth to cool her face; drew off her sleeping clothes and lifted fresh robes onto her shoulders; released her long hair from its ribbons and combed through it; dusted her nose, cheeks, and forehead with white powder; tamped on fresh mothwing eyebrows; and rubbed red on her lips. Taking a large fan, Aoi set off down the corridor for the main hall. The whole house was dark except for the rays of light from the lantern swaying in O-hana's hand.

The hall was a cave of shadows. Two figures showed against a texture of faint light that sifted through the blind behind them. Aoi, moving on her knees, bowed and made a vague melody of politenesses as she approached.

"This is Lady Aoi." The minister's voice came from one of the dark figures. For some reason this meeting was to be held without light. O-hana had left her lamp outside the door. The night beyond the blind was only a small degree less dark than the room.

"Ah yes," said the other voice, which Aoi could not yet identify. "I have heard of you, lady."

"I hope only favorably," said Aoi.

"They feel very close to you at the palace, I think."

"Lady Aoi," said the minister, "is that rare person who understands many things she never expounds."

"I had not thought—" said the other voice.

"—to have a third party witness our talk?" said the minister. "But I have asked this kind lady to help me receive you."

He stopped speaking and Aoi took her cue to offer wine in small cups and bean sweets on individual plates from a tray O-hana had set beside her. O-hana and the guard withdrew and closed the sliding doors.

"Thank you," said the voice, and there were small drinking noises. Aoi's eyes were adjusting to the darkness and she could see that the minister did not raise his own cup. Because he did not speak, the other voice went on after a pause. "I give you too much trouble, coming so late."

"Some urgent matter?" the minister said.

"Urgent, yes. But I come privately, you understand. We have worked closely together for a long time and I felt that I should . . . warn you. That is why I don't wish to be seen." He sighed. "You have sent us your resignation. We—that is, I—hope you only make a gesture. It is true that the council is at the moment lacking in diligence and indulging in rumors, but . . ."

"My resignation is sincerely meant. I tire . . ."

"Ah."

"And your warning?"

"I am afraid—"

Strong footsteps in the hall beyond the closed doors caused the visitor to stop speaking. They all turned as the doors opened and light streamed in, showing them a man bowing, his rounded back stretching the scarlet rep of a short coat, his black cap, his gleaming bound-up hair vivid in the sudden light. He raised himself and faced them, hands on his knees. It was a captain of the Palace Guards.

"Akimitsu?" he said, peering into the room. "You are here already."

So the visitor was the other minister's secretary and the man who sent love notes on gray paper. Light from the hall showed Aoi a slender figure, tall, the features flat and without expression, eyebrows raised. He looked at the captain as if from great height. "It is for private discussion that I am here. You see"—he turned to the minister and lowered his voice—"it is this I meant to warn you about."

The minister widened his eyes. "And you, Captain," he said. "Do you come to see me privately too or is your visit official?"

The captain would not be drawn into polite exchange. His voice took on the singsong of pronouncement, his eyes lost focus so he would not have to see the minister's face. "I come to arrest a traitor who plots against his government—"

"Careful what you say!" The minister's voice was sharp.

"But there is evidence." The captain took a fold of paper from the breast of his uniform. "We have a letter. This is your writing, this is your seal?" He could not help pleading his own reasonableness in believing what had been proved to him.

"With the priests crying plot and overthrow, you know how nervous we have all become, but there must be some mistake," Akimitsu was saying as the paper was opened, read, and passed to Aoi. "Surely you meant some other thing than what that letter appears to say."

"Can one misinterpret the naming of a meeting place, the phrase 'settle final details'?" The captain tried to harden himself.

"I deny that I ever wrote such a letter. Yet I must admit that it looks like my writing and my seal." The minister laughed before turning with serious and intent face to the captain. "This is your proof? This forged letter?"

"A forged letter does not bear the writer's true seal."

"Seals can be forged as well, but I would need good daylight to show you the faults."

"There are no faults, we too have thought of that." Akimitsu's voice was apologetic.

"Genson," said the captain. "He has warned us that his divinings tell of a plot to destroy the government. He has been most agitated and upset for weeks now, knowing the danger."

"Genson, is it? A great creator of danger is Genson. And who else has divined this intended revolution? Ah-h—" raging now and aiming his voice at Akimitsu, "does all my long history of good faith disappear from your minister's weak wits, is getting an heir in the palace so dear to him that he comes to this?"

Akimitsu's face smoothed and he bowed, saying that he must leave now. Aoi, watching from the side, saw his eye gleam. He bowed to the captain with a soft graceful turn of the neck and was gone.

The minister's anger seemed to have solidified the captain's composure, allowing him to draw righteousness about himself. He turned and signaled with a nod of his head. Two guards approached but were held away by the strength of the minister's self-possession. He shifted his whole body and spoke to Aoi. "It seems that these pitiably gullible persons will separate us, just as I was feeling we might become close again."

"You are mistaken," said the captain. "She goes with you."

The minister turned on him. "What outrage is this?"

"But I cannot leave the princess," Aoi said in a voice rough with shock.

"She has other ladies, ladies who do not know poisons and dangerous medicines."

Aoi felt her being compress to the small limits of her skin encased in flimsy silks, as the strange world of isolation she was about to enter flared huge and clanging around her. They both rose and were surrounded and pressed forward by guards who entered from the hall. The captain turned his back and walked on stiff legs ahead of them all. A plain carriage waited at the gate.

"I must speak to her," Aoi said, turning back. Two guards grasped her arms and half-lifted her off the stepping stool and into the bare interior. The minister, already braced against the front gate, put out his hand to steady her. But before she could reach him, the ox was whipped and the carriage started off with a lurch that threw her backward onto the floor. The world below the clouds was not to be cold and distant but hot, painful, and felt against the very skin. The minister's hand in hers was the most actual reality Aoi had ever experienced.

Chapter 12

Many strange things happened just after the banishment of the Great Minister of the Right. The princess, wakened by a servant as soon as the invading guards were gone, ran in her bare feet into the roadway looking for the carriage that had taken her father away. Without making a sound, her robes open and streaming behind, her divided skirt held up to her knees, she ran in the direction the servants indicated, finally stumbling and falling into a heap in the dust. Her women, running after her, had to carry her home.

The prince had not slept that night at the minister's house nor was he in his own mansion when the red-uniformed guards came for him. He was in the secret small house with a young woman from the palace. Steady knocking of the blind against a post, as if the wind swayed it, waked him, and finally he got up to muffle the sound with a cushion.

"And so it is true," said a voice. "A man may be moved by irritation."

The prince, used to intrigue, knelt on the floor

beside the blind, putting his ear close. "Combmaker? You have followed me here?"

"No, but I knew where to find you. For days now we have known where you were—all of you—throughout the days and nights."

"Hunh. And I had thought I lived privately."

"In private danger, that's coming looking for you. Your father-in-law is banished."

"When? I have heard nothing."

"You hear it now. It is very fresh news, they took him only an hour ago."

"And they will send me too?"

"They plan to remove you, yes. To a life of hell."

"Without the minister my life will suffer, wherever I am." He turned back to see if his companion had waked. She still breathed in the light, easy rhythm of sleep. "So. My poor wife. I cannot go to her?"

"You would go into the arms of—"

"The guards?"

"The priests. They will force you to take vows."

The prince did not stop to retrieve discarded clothes. He stepped down from the verandah just as he was and followed the Combmaker to a lacquer shop, where he lived for weeks in the pungent smells of sanded hinoki and cedar wood, of hemp and glue, deer's horn and oil, and lacquer sap both raw and drying.

The emperor, now in smaller rooms, was miserable enough with painful eyes and loss of vision, but the clamor of constant prayers, the ringing of bells and calls to the gods to save him kept him from sleeping until, desperate for quiet, he ordered all the priests into a distant building in the grounds of the temple. He had faithful guards and the priests were afraid of them. Promised lavish refreshment after such strenuous all-night services, they explained to each other that they should organize and concentrate their efforts, and at last they moved, becoming quieter and quieter as the distance from the royal person increased. They ate, they drank a lot of wine, and most of them slept, leaving one poor young priest to keep up the chanting.

It was one of the guards who asked to speak privately with the emperor. He found him lying down. An elderly woman, former nurse to his sons, sat beside him, wringing out white cloths in cool water and laying them across his eyes.

"I should not disturb you," the guard said, "but . . ."

The nurse frowned at him. "Be quick, if you must bother him now."

The emperor raised his hand to quiet her. He recognized the voice of a man who was a private source of information. Always surrounded by chamberlains, councillors, and priests who told him only what they chose, the emperor depended on the Minister of the Right and on this man of the guards to give him the truth of events and of public sentiment.

"The great blue fish," said the man, "has been forced into the fishweir."

"Unh?"

"In the night. They entered his house and took him away."

"On whose orders?"

"It is said that the paper bore the seal of the Minister of the Left. He did not go himself but Akimitsu was there, though the guards claim he went to warn and not to ensure that they got their hands on him. There is feeling against Akimitsu."

"That will not last long. The other minister would be helpless without his secretary. But does he think that he alone . . . ?" The emperor groaned and raised himself, throwing off the wet cloth and groaning again at the pain the light gave him. "Give me paper." Shielding his eyes, squinting to see, he wrote an imperial summons to the Minister of the Left. Then he waited all day but the minister did not come.

The emperor had been thinking that perhaps it would be safe to retire and leave the government in the hands of the Minister of the Right. But now he saw how they had tricked him. If he had properly evaluated the implications of Genson's wild predictions of revolution, he thought, he might have suspected this plot. Now that he understood it, even final blindness would not make him leave.

Taira Munemori had borrowed a house for use during his stay in the capital. His relatives were afraid to have him visit among them, not only because of his reputation for unlawful exploits but because of the number of men he had brought. Feeding them might be possible, they had said, but keeping them from mischief—a great bunch of provincials like that— would not. The courtyard of the borrowed house, always full of horses, was this day also crowded with baggage. Soon they would all be gone and the owners could begin to clean up and make repairs. The men, impatient to return to Shimosa, could not understand why they must wait, and he did not explain. The maids had long since run away and when the visitor's carriage arrived at the gate, there was no one to greet him. A thin old man stepped down and walked to the gallery, dodging and shrinking away among the animals and the sudden jostlings of restless men. He was cross.

The house inside was in terrible disorder, furniture broken and piled in corners, trash on the floors, the straw platform in the main hall cut with a long slash through the matting. Munemori, when the old man found him, was in a small room of the western wing, playing backgammon with his aide. He was not a large man but everything about him was hard—muscles in tight planes and cords, hands and feet callused, jaw bony under dark skin, eyes so insolent the old man almost stumbled. But his anger carried him upright to the last moment before cursory politeness forced him to kneel and bow.

"It is done," he said. "You can take yourself off."

"It is not for your permission I have waited, Uncle."

"You don't think I would drag a box of gold all the way in here, do you? My men have it, in the carriage."

Munemori signaled to the aide, who left the room.

"I don't know what they are thinking of. You will be off building ships now, I suppose, risking your skin to sail to Silla across the sea or making a nuisance of yourself along the coast with your raids on government storehouses. And people will be asking me about it, as if I—"

"I may surprise you. Trade is good, if you can beat the winds and the pirates. And I mean to beat them. What will you say when the whole clan is rich because of me? Already, Uncle, you have your share of this—"

"I will not speak of it."

"But you will accept the income from fifty households which they have given you."

The old man chewed on his lip. "Don't let me see you here again. Stay in Shimosa, or better yet, stay on the sea, sail to China. Family ties have stretched to breaking this time."

"It is my duty to thank you."

"I wish I had done less to help you." The old man stood, with several pauses to prop his bones into position and complete his movements. At the door he made a final bow, twisting his face into a bitter smile. "Watch your back on your way."

Riders and pack animals filled the narrow streets as Munemori led his men south. Not for him the broad avenues, procession and display were not his style. His uncle's warning had been unnecessary, he always kept his men close about him. Yet in two days he was dead from castor bean powder in his stew, and the box of gold disappeared with the cook, whom they had thought a halfwit. Later, when the story was known, it was said that this was the first time the fish symbol was seen: a tiny blue glass fish was left in the empty bowl.

The other minister came home to his wife that evening brimming with seriousness and weighted with responsibility. She had her ladies serve him wine in several small bottles before he was recovered enough to discuss the day's events.

"I believe that I have nearly used up all my voice today," he said after drinking and clearing his throat and drinking again. "So many upsets, so many details to see to, conferences, plans. Without me to give the orders we could never have settled the royal person in his new home. I have had to prepare the crown prince for certain possibilities and we have moved him to a more suitable residence. He is a sweet boy, very teachable, very . . . Well, he is a little upset just now and he misses his rowdy grooms and his cousins who played kickball with him and kept him amused. No more of that, I said. He must live now with dignity. To tell you the truth, he sulked. Oh I am exhausted."

A lady poured more wine, held up for him the plate of pickled fish, the rice bowl, the grilled eggplant. "The other minister," his wife said. (In this house "the other minister" referred to the princess's father.) "The servants say he was treated rudely. They say—"

"You have no need of servants' tales, I am here to tell you the truth about everything. Do you imagine that I would allow any disrespect to my colleague? He has left for some unknown place where he will meditate and pray."

"But why did he go so late at night?"

"You know his modesty, he would not want to make a show."

"And Lady Aoi has gone with him? I always thought he had a feeling for her."

"Lady Aoi? That woman who was lately pushing medicines at the emperor? I know nothing of her. I hope you have not been friendly with her, it would be unwise for us to know such a person."

A lady-in-waiting rose to speak to a maid who came to the door. "There is a visitor," she said, and "Ah!" for the visitor had come right behind the maid.

He refused a cushion and sat on the bare floor, a thin monk wearing rough clothes of dull colors, who wrinkled his nose at the offer of food, reminding them that eating was only for the morning in the religious orders. "But send something to the man who waits for me with the carriage," he said.

The women, who had covered their faces when he came in, left the room, taking the remains of the meal with them. The minister began to bow only halfway, but hearing a hiss of breath from the priest, dropped his head almost to the floor.

"Ah, Genson. Are your predictions more hopeful today?"

"I see a peaceful, well-managed reign, with this treasonous person gone. We have moved just in time to save the government."

"Let us be thankful for divine guidance. It is fortunate too that I am willing to destroy my health in loyal service. I have exhausted myself today, exhausted . . . I hope you can be brief."

"I have come just to say that he will not be back."

"Ah, he is an honorable man who will content himself with religion, I expect, recognizing that his days ripen toward their end."

"That is one way of saying it," said the priest with a twist of his mouth. "Another way is that we will make sure . . ."

"Yes, give him every comfort and he will have no more thoughts of the capital."

"And now there are certain adjustments." The priest spoke for quite a while, the minister nodded and nodded and thought what a rude man, to come so late bothering a person burdened with duties, thought that this Genson took rather a lot on himself, and that really he was not very likable. The other minister became quite irritated.

The princess and those left with her were soon made aware that the house was watched. Guards in the uniform of police stood at every gate and at the corners of the walls, though no one was blocked from going in or out. In the afternoon the official watchers were withdrawn but the servants saw that less conspicuous ones took their places. The gloom in the house was actual as well as spiritual because as the day progressed rain fell from the dreary sky.

The princess, after the first break of control, was miserably silent. Again her husband was not with her at a time of crisis, but she assumed that he too had been taken for banishment. The uncertainties of the safety of her most loved family and of her favorite lady so occupied her mind that she could not join in as her ladies discussed the particulars of what O-hana had overheard. Most outrageous to them was the idea that anyone could believe the minister had ever joined in a plot or written a treasonous letter.

"I would not have thought Akimitsu would insult him by believing in that letter," said Lady Takumi with a glance at Lady Miyuki.

"We can't blame this lady for her friend's lack of faith," said Lady Omi.

Lady Miyuki moved to speak but turned her head away. She was no longer indifferent but intent on all that was said, though she took no part in the talk.

"Besides," continued Lady Omi, "O-hana says that the minister told him the letter was forged, except . . ."

"Except that it was marked with his seal," said Lady Takumi. "Oh it is all so confusing and unjust!" and she released angry tears.

"Lady Takumi," said the princess, worn out with speculation and lack of sleep, "if you don't stop that noise I will shut you up in the storeroom."

She sent them all away and lay down to rest. Her ladies made her comfortable, then went to their own rooms, walking in a group down the dim corridor of the west wing.

"How I wish someone would come this evening," Lady Takumi said, "any friend who could tell us what people are saying about all this. But no one will dare associate with us. You know the saying: A house where there is trouble is always too far to visit."

They did not answer her. "You though"—she tapped her fan on Lady Miyuki's arm—"you have made yourself distant to your admirer Akimitsu but he is not put off. You have never sent him a line of writing—it is pitiful. Yet the gray notes arrive by the dozen. I think that he visits you too?"

"Don't pry," said Lady Omi gently.

"No, no. I don't mind telling you," Miyuki said. "I have not sent him any writing at all and I have done everything to discourage him. But"—she smiled without warmth, a cold little compression of the corners of her mouth, while her eyes flicked pride and then were cast down—"he comes."

Chapter 13

Until they reached the ferry over the Kadomo River, Aoi and the minister were violently jarred and thrown about within the bare carriage. They could hear guards on horseback urging the running ox driver to whip his animal to more speed. Inside the city the street surfaces were smooth but the road west became rough on the outskirts and the great wheels crashed into holes and rose and fell over rocks and tree roots, tossing the carriage in all directions and encasing the passengers in a grinding racket of sound. All their energy was needed to hold their heads away from the walls and to keep a grip on the wooden struts over which the palm-leaf matting was stretched. Aoi felt that they were no longer persons but goods in shipment.

At the ferry the carriage stopped. Aoi's ears rang in the relative silence, then she could hear men talking, the stump of horses, wind in the trees, and under everything, the rush of water over stones. It was still dark but there was a firebasket near the ferryman's house. This light, seen through the tied-down blind,

meant to Aoi that people were there, the first to see
them as helpless captives. She could not help hoping
illogically that they would protest, that they would
save their minister and his friend.

They did not protest. They did not seem to think it
odd that such a group should come in the middle of
the night and they did not seem to realize who their
passengers were, so closely surrounded by men and
horses as the ferry was poled to the other bank. Aoi
could not cover her face, both hands required again
for bracing against motion. She held on to an empty
stirrup on one side, the minister's arm on the other.
The flat boat rocked and slid on the water, the
breathing mass of the horse, shifting its weight almost
against her shoulder, terrified her, the smell of it
filling her mouth as well as her nose. When, on the
other side, they put her in a saddle, she was nearly
fainting from overwhelming strangeness.

The Captain of the Guards, the same one who had
confronted them in the minister's main hall, made a
formal speech describing the forced journey they
would make. "It is ordered that you travel to far
Kyushu under the harshest conditions. This is mild
punishment for your crime of plotting to destroy the
government. All your guards—" He looked at a large
troop of men without uniforms who had just ridden
up. They were armed, as were the Palace Guards, with
swords and bows. Several of them also held lances.
"—are ordered to obey the conditions that are ordered by order of—" Feeling that his language was
somehow losing force and still not quite master of his
own respect for the minister, the captain stopped.

"You have your orders, yes," said the minister in a
helpful way, sitting easily on his horse, which he was
able to cause to stand perfectly still. Aoi wondered
how he did it; her mount was backing and circling and
she felt that every shift of its legs must tip her off.
"But do tell us whose orders they are."

"Orders are orders." The captain could not seem to
abandon that one word, which he repeated for safety

and to remind himself that he was a man for others to use, that he had no control himself over what was being done. "From my Major Captain." More satisfied now that he had assigned responsibility to a superior, the captain continued, addressing the new guards. "No food or fresh horses are to be allowed."

The minister, startled, involuntarily pulled on the reins and his horse leaped backward. "Over a month on the road with no food?"

"Your horses may graze."

"I will not waste words arguing with you and your orders. But I will tell you one thing. All your life you will take the measure of smallness from what you have done this night."

The minister turned his horse and put his back to the captain, riding up beside Aoi, showing her how to hold the reins, making her pat the vibrant neck so she could begin to feel that this construction of bone and muscle and silky hide that towered so high above the ground might have spirit and sense, might obey her will, and would some day receive her affection and gratitude.

The new guards were practical and uncivil. With hardly a word to anyone, they surrounded their charges and set a fast pace westward under a lightening sky. When it began to rain Aoi and the minister were soon soaked and cold. Aoi fainted and slid from the saddle. They threatened to tie her across the horse's back and she roused, finding in herself anger and forging it into determination not to show weakness. The minister tried to take her on with him but was prevented and they rode until late in the chill and darkening afternoon.

When night came they were told to sleep on the bare ground. The guards gave them no mats or covers. By refusing to speak, the minister was strangely able to keep some authority. When they indicated separate places for the two captives to lie, he grasped Aoi in his arms and turned away to find a high mossy place in the grove of trees where their camp was to be. The

men laughed and hooted to each other but did not
force them to obey. Aoi allowed herself to sink against
the minister's strength and within moments was unconscious.

Waking in the night, she felt his arm still holding
her, his solid bulk warm against her back. Her limbs
seemed locked in their bent position, her head ached,
the places where bone had jolted all day against
saddle throbbed as if the rhythm of the horse still
moved beneath her. She opened her eyes and could
see, surprisingly near, a pile of embers where the
guards must have made a fire for cooking and around
it the sleeping forms of men wrapped in blankets. She
lay still. Stretching out would be sweet release but it
seemed a matter for long thought before she could
decide to move. She did not want to wake the
minister, but most of all she was afraid of losing the
privacy of being, finally, unobserved. The men had
watched her with intensity throughout the day and
one of them had accompanied her into the trees when
she had asked to relieve herself.

The minister woke, tensing against her. They had
not been able to speak to each other since they were
put into the carriage. "I could not have a braver
companion," he said.

"Not brave, enduring."

"I will not live to see Kyushu, I think. But you must
escape."

"I won't leave you." Aoi was surprised to hear
herself say that to the minister. She had always been
fond of him, admiring his fully genuine character that
had no pockets of falseness, self-deceit, pride, venge-
fulness, or posing. They had even, once, been briefly
in love, but had agreed with delectable sad sweetness
that they could not join their lives. Now, however, the
force of happening had put them together and it
seemed a bond of fate. Perhaps their previous parting
had been an insult to their joint karma, which was
now made right. Or perhaps—Aoi felt a wry smile on

her face at the thought—perhaps it was not sentiment but simple dependence and fright that made leaving him now unthinkable. This thought caused her misery and she wondered why she always had to pry into her emotions, analyzing. With more fervor, because she hoped it was true, she said again, "I will not leave you."

"No talking!" The tip of a lance dug into the ground in front of Aoi's face. There had been a guard on duty behind them. Aoi turned into the minister's embrace, hiding her face against his chest. Her throat ached and with all her strength she repressed tears. "Quiet!" The guard spoke in whispered shouts, though they had not said more, except that the minister groaned once. In the morning she saw that he had a wound on the back of his shoulder where the lance had jabbed. The guards did not allow her to dress it.

The road west was heavily traveled. All during the first day the group of armed men and their two prisoners had caused some curiosity but people had seemed not to know them. By the second day, though, the story had spread and everyone they met, farmer, priest, or nobleman, peered after them or altered their path to follow along. Some tried to speak to the minister, some rebuked the guards, many commented on the shamelessness of Aoi's uncovered face or the pity they felt for her. Some people were drawn along behind them by curiosity but most stood off to the side of the road and bowed to show respect. Aoi could see that the minister, though he kept his face impassive, was heartened that the accusation of treason was not universally believed.

In the late morning they arrived at a post town. The road passed between houses of dark weathered wood and wound uphill to the stables, pens, and pastures of the post station. All the guards dismounted, walking about, flexing their limbs, calling for food and drink. The minister and Aoi were not allowed any of these luxuries and sat high on their horses among the milling men and animals. Apparently they would not be allowed to change their mounts.

The townspeople who gathered about were afraid of the guards and hostile to the man of the government who was their prisoner, glad to see him in disgrace and sullen with unspoken resentment. Looking at their patched clothes and their undernourished children, at the women bent and sun-scorched, Aoi wondered why they did not rebel against the heavy taxes of rice, craftwork, and conscripted labor that she knew oppressed them. Only her present condition of helplessness allowed her to realize the unjust basis of the refined life she and all the others led above the clouds. She knew also now what helplessness was.

One of the women who stood watching turned to her husband and murmured, "Won't they even give these poor people—" Though her voice had been low, a guard heard her and struck her in the side with his sword, not cutting but crushing ribs with the flat of the blade. She began to howl and was silenced and taken away by her family.

"Give them water," said one of the guards. He was an old man and Aoi had seen him walk with a limp. His stiff gray hair stuck up all over his head, escaped from a loose topknot that was equally unruly and upright, and he had a fondness for flourishing his sword, swiping at grass, and sometimes whirling it around his head to hear it sing. That morning he had made a mock attack on the minister, hoping to make him cringe. His eyes swung wildly and Aoi was frightened of him, though he had never approached her. This guard, holding out his arms and turning from side to side to be sure he was observed, dipped his mug in the horse trough and held it up to Aoi, saying in a loud voice, "Drink, witch!" and to the people of the town, "She is a medicine witch, this one."

Aoi would have reached for the water, foul as it was, but the man threw it in her face. The minister turned his horse and rode at the guard, who whipped out his sword and put the point of it against the horse's chest. "Won't you have some too?" he said, and scooped and threw rapidly from the surface of the tank again and again until the minister was drenched.

Some of the older men of the stables ran to change saddles and gear to the fresh horses as fast as possible but the guards lolled against the fence and on the steps of the herders' quarters with their rice cakes and bamboo mugs of wine, displaying their power to delay as long as they pleased.

One of them looked about and said to the man beside him, "These people make me ashamed. What would it hurt to feed them a little rice? Look at them."

Hearing this, Aoi turned her head toward the minister, at the same time bending, as he did, with pain caused by the thought of food. The minister's clothes were stained with dirt and with green from the moss where they had slept, and there was blood on his shoulder. Though his cap was dented and bent, the forehead under it was smooth and he allowed himself no expression. His eyes watched the speaker.

"Fool," the guard's companion said without interest, "he has taken the rice from many a farmer who starves his family to pay him land tax."

"Unh." The speaker slid his eyes toward a third guard, who had been listening. Aoi became giddy, her ears rang, and black spots shifted across the view of houses and mountains beyond. By the time she had control of her balance, they were moving again. She dropped the reins and gripped both hands into the horse's mane.

Aoi knew nothing of the afternoon. Only when they stopped to camp did she realize that she had ridden while asleep, arms and legs rigid to hold her in place. She was surprised to find that the wild-eyed old guard had the reins of her horse and was leading it. At the camping place beside a stream, he threw the reins at her, saying with spasmed face, "Witch!" and riding to the opposite side of the clearing before dismounting.

Chapter 14

In spite of their exhaustion and physical pain, Aoi and the minister did not lie down to sleep as soon as the camp was made. Aoi had dreamed as she slept while riding, dreamed of the most pungently fragrant food she knew, broiled boar. Now similar odors came to them in the smoke from the guard's fire and hunger kept them sitting up in their sleeping place. Though they could have eased their bodies, they stretched toward every wafting smell of meat, bellies knotted.

The man guarding them stepped away to fill his food bowl, his place taken by another, who squatted on the ground almost beside Aoi. The new guard held his full bowl under his chin and poised his chopsticks, but looked at the prisoners and lowered his hands.

"Excuse me," he mumbled and shifted his feet without rising until he had shuffled some distance away. Looking toward them, he raised the bowl, waved the chopstick hand in apology, and prepared again to eat. The smell of meat and onion was making Aoi faint and she swayed.

The guard dropped his jaw, looked into his bowl,

inhaling its aroma, and back toward the captives who had not eaten for two days. His shoulders slumped, his whole body went slack, and he shook his hanging head. In sudden frenzy, he shuffled toward Aoi, holding out the bowl of meat and vegetables for her to take. Ducking his head again, he said, "Seeing you like this, I cannot eat," and with incoherent grunts he thrust the bowl upward. Aoi recognized the voice of the guard who had wanted to give them rice at the post town.

Her hands leaped to receive the bowl and she turned to offer it to the minister too. But he struck it from her and she watched as the food spilled and the bowl bounded into the darkness.

Looking steadily at the guard, the minister held Aoi's arm in his warm hand and moved his forefinger against her skin to comfort her. The guard was momentarily infuriated but controlled his face and sauntered back to the fire as the man he had replaced came back.

"Don't trust them," the minister said under his breath.

"No talking!" roared the guard. His shout brought several others to stand about them and quote their orders, taunting and cold. Loudest of all was the limping old man, who capered so that he got in the way of a lance jab aimed at the minister and clapped his hand to his backside, whirling on the one who had stuck him and chasing him into the dark fields outside the grove of trees where the camp was. Laughing, the men returned to the fire and the prisoners began to clear stones from their resting place.

As she had dreamed of food in the afternoon, Aoi dreamed in the night of soft floss-filled sleeping pads from which she continually fell onto a hip-bruising hard cold floor. The smell of fish intruded and she thought she recognized the other longing that followed her into sleep. It was a not ideally appetizing smell but so strong that she woke and felt the minister

too tighten his muscles. Still there was the fish smell
and now taste, as a morsel of fish flesh was pressed
against her lips, making her jaws ache, the inside of
her mouth burn, and her throat close.

"Fish," a voice said behind Aoi's head, as a man
bent to whisper to the minister. "Wherever you see
fish it is safe. Remember that. You are the Great Blue
Fish, we are your people." And Aoi felt the oily flakes
of a slice of smoked eel in her hand. She would have
pushed it all into her mouth at once but the pain of
the first surge of appetite was too great and she made
several bites of it.

"Give me the bones." Aoi wanted to keep the
section of backbone for the taste, but she removed it
with her fingers and put it into a hand waiting beside
her cheek. The man rose, walked a few paces, and
sprayed urine into the field, then went back to his post
on guard behind them. They knew nothing of him
except his whispered voice and his rough palm.

Aoi turned to lie facing the minister and gripped his
hands. They did not speak. Breaking that rule might
cause trouble for the guard who had fed them. As if
emerging from mist, Aoi found herself exploring the
rational powers of her own mind. Despair drew away
and she saw only now how limiting it had been. The
energy of planning, so long absent, livened her brain
and passed healing to her body, vibrating through her
hands to the minister. His own awakened hope passed
to her.

"We," the man had said. "We are your people."

Aoi found in her mind a few certainties, fixed
landmarks. She toured them all.

The letter said to be proof of the minister's guilt
was a forgery.

The minister had been removed by false accusation
so that someone else could advance.

If that someone could be exposed, the minister
would be returned to his position, an honored man
again.

But—solidest and blackest truth of all—he was

meant to die on this journey. Even with help from secret friends, he might not survive.

An ally in the capital was needed, a person who could find the plotter and prove a case against him.

Aoi herself was such a person.

Therefore . . . She hesitated before the frightening mass of her conclusion. Therefore she, Aoi, must escape.

The minister had made this circuit of logic on the first day and come to the same decision. Her hands loosened on his as a wave of physical fear pulled through her, but he shook her gently and touched her face in a gesture of trust and she gave up the luxury of dread. Lightened, she fell asleep against his arm.

Aoi had always had a tendency to regard thought as physical, a strength that could be flexed and developed through exercise. Observation—silent attentive use of the eyes and of moral receptors—was the nourishment of thought, and tracing the shapes of pattern its skilled performance. It was not with weariness that she bent her mind on the following day to the problem of living into a future she could to some extent control. She felt mentally rested and fit, alive to the day and all its details.

Rifts of cloud were pigeon colored at sunrise and there was a steady wind, scuttling dry leaves against the roots of trees. It was cold but Aoi was too busy to notice because there were so many things to see and she had been so blind until now.

The men were breaking camp, heaving lumpy bundles onto the pack horses, smacking the bellies of their mounts so the girths tightened properly, stamping and beating their arms to warm themselves, shaking their coats and belting them. They wore no common uniform. Whose men were they? In their faces was no refinement, but high birth was not a requirement for warriors. Their weapons were similar, all the swords with handles wrapped in black thong, all the lance tips cut to the same shape. In age they varied from youths to the gray-haired old man.

Their speech was low, bare of the politenesses usual in the familiar talk of the men Aoi knew. But these guards were probably of the provinces, where everything was different.

Which of them had brought the eel? It would not be wise to try too hard to identify him but watching might give her a clue.

On the road again, riding the horse that, as much as she feared it, had never failed in steadiness, she was alert. The fields were dry, striped with tan stubble. Near the villages, racks of rice sheaves leaned together in pointed rows. Men passed with loads of firewood huge on their backs, children walking barefoot behind them, also balancing spiky bundles. Women in kerchiefs came out of the doors of distant houses and crossed to join other women. Dogs became hysterical and were dragged away as the procession of horses approached.

One of these unknown persons might show the fish sign, offer help, food, a chance to get away. Aoi was watchful but concealed it. Glancing at the minister, she saw him as impassive as ever, in his usual mode of attention.

Since she herself was now observing, she felt less the object of the eyes of the men, as if her own will to see protected her. She was strengthened by the secret she knew, by the hope it gave her.

A squat broad-necked guard pushed his horse against her, crowding, his leg in its wrappings rubbing against hers, which was covered only with her thin hot-weather robes. As he shoved past, his hand roughened the silk on her thigh, then slapped, and he was gone. It was done secretly, not with showy bravado, and Aoi was abruptly frightened. She would have preferred public jeering.

The night was to be spent in another post town. The guards appropriated the hostlers' quarters and Aoi and the minister were taken to separate rooms and locked in, still without any food or bedding. Deprived of the stimulation of activity and scenery, Aoi was attacked by acute physical misery and she rattled the door and begged for water. The guard outside—she knew there would be one—grunted no. There was silence for a long time. Darkness became complete. The floor of the room was gritty and colder than the ground. Aoi had never felt so mortal, had never so resented the vulnerable casing of her mind and spirit. She thought that tears would be a relief but found they did not come just because she would allow them and she was too tired to thrash up emotion on purpose. Her body ached, her insides stirred and bit. The longing for food and water were so strong that she feared she would never be free of them. She hallucinated dishes and dishes of great variety and fragrance, imagined herself tasting delicately, picking with chopsticks here and there, savoring, inhaling, sipping, eating for hours and never full. She slept.

Afterward she thought of it as a matter of weight. It was his heavy hand on her throat that waked her, his massive knee between her legs that kept her from rising, his fist swung like a block of lead into her side that silenced her cry, his ponderous clumsiness in lowering himself that allowed her to roll partway over and escape his stabbing organ. She tried to shout as she turned but there was so little breath left in her that the sound was slight, rising and choked off, so much like a sigh of passion that Aoi ground her teeth and forced growling noises into her throat. Thick fingers splayed against her face, blocking nose and mouth. There was a space of stillness. When she tried to reach the hand, the grind of bone against plank echoed in the bare room. His breath was loud and he smothered it. He pulled his hand into her hair and drew his knife with a slithering metallic sound.

"Hunh." He waited. She was quiet, not moving.

He felt into her layers of robes. Alien, cold as lizard skin, his fingers pressed and kneaded, squeezed until she arched suddenly, pinched to be sure she would not use her voice. The tip of the knife prodded into the skin under her ear.

Again he lowered himself. Aoi felt the bulk of his sex and a sudden thrust against her bare hip. His excitement had betrayed him and he wrenched her hair for it, not knowing he pulled her away from the knife point.

She heard the door slide in its track. "Playing, are we?" said a voice, and bare feet bumped and brushed the floor, too many sounds for one man to make. Ice crisped hard under Aoi's ribs. The man sat up away from her and she drew herself into a ball, hiding, not wanting to know how many now squatted around her in the dark. There were prods, pulls at her clothes, high-vibrating smothered laughs. And all at once, light.

"Put out that—" One of the squatting men dived sideways to take the lantern. He was met with a straight arm that struck his jaw.

"No, no. I want to watch."

"You think, old man, to get your pleasure—"

"Have you touched her yet?" He looked at the thick man who held the knife still aimed at Aoi's throat.

"You might call it touching. I call it something else." He smoothed the folds of his wrapped pants over his groin. "Several times I . . . touched her."

"Ah, well," said the old guard. "Too bad for you."

"Hunh. I'm the smart one, I got here first."

"Smart? When it falls off you won't think you're so smart."

Aoi, only now able to sort out the confusion of feet and legs around her, saw three men draw away from the one at her side. The knife point fell with a thud into the floorboards. No one spoke.

"Don't you know this one is a witch? They put something inside themselves and . . . Even the sweat of a witch can rot your flesh."

The guard who had attacked her grabbed at himself, then clearly thinking he might have been too strong, cradled his scrotum and backed away. He did not pick up the knife.

"Aren't you going to let us see?" sounded after him as he left the room.

"He should count his fingers, too," the old man explained in a kindly way to the other three. "Who's next?" But he spoke now to their backs.

When they were all gone, the old man slid the door shut again and pinched out the wick in its basin of oil. Aoi heard him shuffling and his voice sounded next against her ear. "What fools. Now they've left you for me. And I have a charm against witches."

He made a few fumbling gropes against her clothes but then pushed her hip, rolling her over to lie facedown, and he stood.

"Sleep, witch. I'm too old and I've had this charm too long to trust it. I may not be able to use this thing," he said to himself as he moved toward the door, "but I still need it."

Her breath shuddering, Aoi searched the entire floor for the fallen knife. It was gone but in a corner were a large section of bamboo filled with water and a wad of leaf folded over cold rice. She could feel in the dark that a fish bone lay on it and she ate and drank.

Chapter 15

Aoi did not count the days but they traveled for a
while before she observed any change that had meaning. There were long hours of riding, campsites, post
towns, food and water provided in unexpected ways
and by unknown persons. The minister was continually abused with kicks and jabs but no one touched
Aoi. She heard one of the guards tell another that if he
let his lance come in contact even with her clothes, it
would turn against his own breast. Though she was
careful not to be exactly threatening, Aoi kept her
expression solemn and her eyes direct, thinking that
she should take whatever advantage she could of their
belief in her powers and giving herself the air of
considering whether to use them. Any man assigned
to go with her into the woods for the needs of nature
kept her at a wide distance and hid himself behind a
tree until she returned. Once she tried stealing away in
the opposite direction, but the guard was not so afraid
of her that he would let her escape. He called out,
nocked an arrow into his bow, and she returned.
Afterward, the guard spread the wisdom that an

arrow was the proper weapon against a witch and when they wanted to coerce her, they drew their bows.

Then she noticed that their way had turned south. This meant that part of the journey would be made on the Inland Sea. It meant boats, change, confusion, and possibly the splitting of the guards into smaller groups. She looked at the minister and then at the lowering sun, which they now saw on their right sides. He let his eyelids drop a fraction to show that he understood.

The minister's condition worried Aoi. Not only was he weakened by lack of food and drink, but his shoulder wound seeped. There was a cut over one eye where a thrown rock had hit him in one of the towns, and she knew he had taken many blows from fists and the butts of lances. Though he kept his silence and through it some dignity, he sometimes reeled in the saddle.

They came to a river where the crossing was deep. There were arguments about who would lead Aoi's horse and the duty was given to the old man, though he protested. When finally forced to take the reins, he wrapped a cloth around his hand.

To Aoi's disappointment, the water came barely to the horse's belly. She longed to drink and to lave her face, and she reached down with one hand and scooped water into her mouth. It was so cold it burned but she reached for more. The old man was wrestling his horse, which disliked the cold, and he did not notice. Ahead of her, the minister's horse suddenly stumbled and he fell into the river on the downstream side. Seeming to be unconscious, the minister began to float away. He was easily retrieved but when they laid him out on the grass of the bank, he did not stir. Aoi slid from the horse so hastily that she fell. Because the men were afraid to touch her, she reached the minister, turned him facedown, saw water gush from his mouth, and felt him begin to shiver.

After confused discussion, the guards decided to

camp where they were. Aoi managed to clean the minister's shoulder wound with a corner of his wet robe and she warmed him as he slept.

They came to another river at the end of the next day and paced the horses through a wide sandy ford, within sound of the sea. The horses wet their mouths cautiously; the captives were offered a drink but they knew from the sarcastic manner of the guard who held the cup that the water was brackish and they refused it.

Soon after the ford they entered a fishing village where a few houses circled a round cove that was protected from the open sea by a long spit of land, a slender arc where stunted pines grew. The channel was anchored on the opposite side by tall craggy rocks, also crowned with a fringe of little bent pines. All the boats had come in for the night and were pulled high on the beach. From her horse Aoi could see the two endless planes of gray sea and gray sky separated by a band of light at the horizon, dull wrinkled surface of water breaking into froth around many small black islands and inverted billows of cloud rolling above. After she dismounted she saw only the tipping choppy peaks of the water in the cove and the rickety color-stripped houses with their high porches and uneven ladders.

Fishing village. Fishermen. Fish.

Even the guards seemed to feel awe in this place of wide shelving beach and heavy sky, the village and the pines frail challenging proppings between. Wind streamed steadily against them, water lapped and splashed close at hand and roared where the long waves broke onto rock outside the harbor. Quieter than she had ever seen them, elbows out to make themselves wider but hunched over as if to pass safely in a low place, the group of armed men rode into the village.

The fishermen stood by their boats, still winding nets or securing gear or just holding the top strakes as if to protect their means of living. No one greeted the strangers. Women pulled their children indoors, then leaned their heads out to look, headcloths pulled close. An old man with a withered arm stepped sideways down the ladder from his house and walked to meet them. For the first time one guard put himself forward as leader. Aoi wondered that she had not identified him before but all decisions had been made by loud discussion and final agreement and she had not been aware that anyone issued orders. This leader who now rode out alone was actually one of the quieter ones, of slight build and neat appearance.

He dismounted to approach the village headman on foot and even bowed slightly. Their conference was brief, heads together, backs to the wind. The old man nodded and, seeing that, the fishermen came to lead away the horses.

Aoi realized that she was sliding down for the last time from what had seemed at first a dangerous height. The animal's broad shifting back was familiar to her, the rise and fall of its haunches under her seat had been a life connected to her own during long days. She felt pity for it as a being not free, for its hardships and for her own. Tears she would normally have suppressed wet her face and she let herself fall against the warm tense fragrant sheen of its shoulder, stroking with one hand, pulling her dirty robes to her chest with the other, cold from the wind, afraid of changing even such bleak routine, robbed of her identity and feeling too weak and beset to make the new person she felt would soon be required.

Something was not right with the minister. He was smiling. He sank down smiling on the sand and looked about. Sunset behind the village reflected pink color even into the east beyond the spit and the water shimmered rose and blue. Smoothing his hands from side to side on the beach, the minister bent forward to gaze through the opening where the channel was. When they pulled him to his feet, he hung limp between two of them and was carried by his arms and dumped under one of the houses. Aoi ran toward him.

But the guards trained arrows on her and she went where they indicated, up the steps and into a storehouse. The slam of the door echoed, the wooden bolt rattled and dropped.

Except for dried fish hanging in dense rows from the rafters, the storehouse was empty. The thick oily smell was almost nourishing but the fish themslves were out of her reach and the frustration of being in the presence of so much unobtainable food made Aoi weep again. Who was to hear, in this place of wind and surf? Finally completely isolated, she cried. And cried. Until her mind drew away and thought detached itself from her emotions, puzzling first about the minister's strange behavior on the beach, connecting this house full of fish with the sign that always meant help, and finally worrying and prying at the question of how to get a fish down from above. Aoi cried on, as if in a helpless physical condition of illness, while the solution came. A pole. There must be a pole here to prop open the air hole in the roof. Still streaming tears and gasping sobs, she felt about in the corners. Yes. Here it was.

Rather than detaching, the fish broke apart when struck with the pole, but she knocked down quite a few and ate until she was full, a sensation that almost made her weep again for the long absence of it. Before she allowed herself to sleep, she swept together all the debris from her eating and crammed it into the corner least likely to be lit by light when the door opened in the morning.

They came for her just after dawn and led her to the beach. A large boat with a sail had come to anchor in the harbor during the night and the smaller boats of the fishermen were already being rowed back and forth with supplies. Some of the guards were on board, careful of their handholds, laughing to each other about trying to put their feet down on a deck that tipped away under them. If they had to move across the deck, they crept with outstretched arms, never letting go of ropes or rails. The upended backside of one of them was visible hung over the far rail as he lost his breakfast into the waves. Aoi saw the minister lifted over the side, as she herself was rowed across the choppy bay. The little boat she was in rose and fell several times beside the hull of the larger one until the fishermen had the rhythm of it and one of them raised her bodily on a crest and a crew member above grasped her arms and swung her to the deck. She was taken at once to the lattice-covered cabin in the stern. The minister was not in sight and she assumed he had been put in some space below the deck.

Finally all the men seemed to be aboard but someone was missing. Aoi understood from what she could hear that it was the pilot for whom they waited. Shut in a small space she began to feel unwell. The boat vibrated against the anchor rope, shuddering and twisting.

With shouts and laughter from several men, the pilot's boat arrived. Aoi heard jovial apologies and remarks about not missing the dawn wind and watching out for the reefs among the islands. She identified a woman's voice and was surprised.

"For good fortune on your journey," the woman said.

"Wah! Such a huge fish!"

"Best omen of all," said a man, "is a fish given by a pregnant woman."

"We are very glad to have your fish"—it was a truculent guard—"but this will be just a quiet trip of no great distance. And we are on the Inland Sea, after all." He laughed and coaxed the others to join him. "We will be in no danger."

"The Inland Sea, but treacherous, treacherous."

"Let us go then, while it is calm. On your way, and be careful you don't slip going over the side."

"What? A fisherman's wife?" The woman had a big laugh.

"Wine!" cried a voice and there seemed to be a surge forward.

"I'll just put this away in here."

The door of Aoi's cabin opened and the pregnant fishwife entered, cradling a monstrous carp wrapped in woven green bamboo leaves. She motioned Aoi to be silent and began to take off her clothes. The pregnancy was a sack of bran chaff tied around her body and the woman was actually a portly man. Waving apology, he indicated that Aoi should remove all but her white under-robe, then he tied the bag around her and tightened the straps, dressed her in the woman's clothes he had removed, and arranged the headcloth so it almost covered her face.

When they opened the door, the old man who had so persecuted Aoi was standing guard. She was taken by the two of them around the free-standing cabin and lifted down to a fishing boat which waited under the stern, sail luffed, spar rattling in the wind. The old man came down after her, the man who had given her the clothes stayed on board. "He's the pilot," the guard explained, as he guided Aoi to a cushion between the thwarts and showed her how to hold on and brace herself. Just as the pilot was about to cast off the line that held them, one of the guards approached. He had one hand on his belly, the other mopped with a cloth the cold sweat on his cheeks.

"Where do you think you're going, old man? We all have to endure this boat and you are not to be spared."

"It took two of us to lower this august woman. I'm coming back aboard. And I won't be sick like you are, I can tell you. Watch out! You almost—"

The fisherman who was to sail the little boat had hold of the rail of the ship and was pulling rhythmically, enlarging the natural motion of the water and nearly throwing the seasick guard overboard. He flailed out a hand to steady himself, finding and grasping the rope that tied the little boat, and pulled low as it sank with the next wave.

"Wait," he said. "That woman doesn't look—" But

the pilot, who had already untied the rope, let it go and the man fell into the sea, still holding on. The old guard watched for a space as their boat gained speed before the wind, dragging the blubbering man behind them. Then he cut the rope and they left him to sink. The guards on the large boat were carousing with morning wine to dull their fear of going on the water and they did not see their companion go overboard.

The little boat carrying Aoi sped for the harbor channel and was soon behind the pillars of black rock. It was quiet now that the sail was taut.

"Won't they catch us?" Aoi asked.

"They will go a long way in the other direction before you are missed."

"Why should the pilot help me?"

"Ah, why should any of us help you? The pilot and the fishermen because this is the minister's village and he is a just landlord."

"You mean they brought us to one of the minister's estates and didn't know it?"

"They are city no-goods and clods from the country, they don't know anything. We led them here."

"We? Then there are more of you? And who are you and these others?"

The old man smiled, looking out to sea, his face relaxed, his rough gray hair pushed forward by the wind. Some smug secrecy in his expression was familiar to Aoi and she understood many things all at once. "Ah," she said, "the Combmaker has sent you." He only looked at her, his job done. "And how did you know where this place was?" she said.

"This was once my village."

"But won't they attack the villagers when they discover . . .?" Aoi, finally able to talk freely, could not stop her questions.

"You must understand about boats. They will be glad to land wherever we land them and it will not be possible for them to come after you."

"And the minister?"

"That will be for later. He knows, he can wait. Didn't you see last night that he recognized the place?"

"I thought he was delirious, that he saw paradise in this watery place with the pink sky."

"It was relief that made him so weak."

"You deceived them all, but you had to deceive us too, or we might have . . . Even in the attack on me in that room . . ."

"Lady, I believe you understand that and you will forgive me."

"Your talk of witches saved me. That is a story the Combmaker will enjoy and my gift to you is that you may be the one to tell it to him." Thinking of seeing the Combmaker again and of all that must happen before then and before she would be able to return to life as she had known it, if she ever could, Aoi became grave. Now that she was free, she had the responsibility of proving the minister's innocence and of exposing the plot against him. How she would do that and stay in hiding at the same time, she had no idea. But for now, the rough clothes of a fisherman's wife were warm and she found comfort in the weight of the bag against her stomach, symbol of rest in the care of others. How easy it had been, after all, to become a new person.

Chapter 16

"You must understand, lady, that you are to have a lover who has hidden you away here in this modest district." The Combmaker, in charge of Aoi's concealment, had brought her to the prince's secret house. Instructing her in deception, an art he understood, he made his voice prim and waved a closed fan at her, all jocular chiding and severity. "This worthless woman"—he broke off to touch the fan to the arm of Aoi's new maid, who was in fact a dimpled girl—"will be here all the time to see that you . . ." The touch of even the end of a fan on such a round young arm seemed to distract him and he leaned toward her, forgetting his lecture, dropping one hand to her knee and edging closer. The girl turned her face away, letting her short hair fall forward as a screen, but with a calm familiar to Aoi. She was O-hana's niece.

"A lover?"

Sighing, he gave the girl a last pat and resumed his explanation of Aoi's role in this crowded section of the Sixth Ward. "We must have a reason, you see, for such a lady as you are—such long hair, so fine-boned, so beautiful—to be living here with only a maid and the woman of the house, and you must be someone's mistress, the usual thing."

"I see that we could joke like this all afternoon but I understand that the lover, as you call him, can be a means of communication. Is he also to be my agent, the one who can move about in the city, carry messages and the like?"

"Lady, you see too quickly." He was complaining. "And you do not shriek and protest, you are just no fun at all."

"Now you are unkind. Didn't I waddle into that temple as a clumsy fat pregnant smelly shuffling gawking fishwife and you paced and fretted at the meeting place and passed me a dozen times, pushing me aside? Didn't I kneel right beside you, when you gave up and sat down, and heave a very convincing groan and clasp my sack of bran chaff and frighten you into the corner behind the war god's statue? Didn't I pen you in that corner and speak the proper dialect as I asked you to help me? Only pity for your stammerings and your perspiring face made me relent and say that some fish slip easily through the teeth of the finest comb."

The Combmaker laughed and told the puzzled girl, who was named Ateki, how Aoi had fooled him. He mimed again his open mouth, his cautious peep under Aoi's headcloth, his choking effort not to laugh and shout, and his quiet meek manner as he helped the bulky woman to the house he had prepared for her. Laughter so severely pent at the time the joke was realized seemed to multiply as it was retold.

"And who is this lover? It must be someone familiar with the court but not too well-known himself," Aoi said.

"Who more familiar than a Fifth Rank Chamberlain who looks to every chance for higher connection to advance himself?"

"Oh please don't send me some aging carping man

still yearning for his boy's job and bitter that he
cannot rise to a post in administration. You know
how vicious they are, how secretive and sly, how they
gossip and . . ."

The Combmaker was nodding. "Exactly."

"Ah yes."

"His name is Sukemasa."

Aoi groaned. "I know him. The one with a scar in
his eyebrow that gives him a disdainful look. Why on
earth should he want to mix himself in this?"

"Genson has offended him. Once when there was a
procession at Todai Temple, Sukemasa was seen to
make a remark to his partner just before they set out
and they both laughed. Genson raged at him for
impiety—oh how he screamed, right there in front of
all the people. Sukemasa turned his face to him—that
peaked eyebrow, that mouth like this"—the Combmaker twisted his lips down on one side—"and said
that such insults to a member of the emperor's
household were blasphemy and treason both and that
a priest should know better. So he put Genson in his
place but Sukemasa is a touchy man who does not
forget."

"Yes, Genson has made an enemy who can be
imaginatively spiteful. There have been others who
thought they could slight Sukemasa. I don't like such
games but now I too must gather secrets and wish
people ill while concealing myself."

"Please, lady, don't be concerned. Sukemasa
knows, I think, that he has never had a more important reason to pretend, to listen, to be charming or to
bully, to walk about at night—oh he always knows
which lady entertains which gentleman and sometimes what their notes to each other say."

"Ah well. It is only to observers that he will be a
lover visiting his lady. Sukemasa has his faults but
lack of understanding of where respect is due is not
one of them. Yet, what would he do if *I* were to offend
him? I am afraid to trust him."

"Whoever it was who sent him to us has pointed

out to him that when the minister is restored to his post, he will promote his loyal friend Sukemasa. It is his only hope because the other minister dislikes him."

"Someone sent him?"

"There are some who do not agree with what the other minister has done. They must be silent or they will lose their positions, but we hear things."

Aoi could no longer pursue the ghostly interleavings of intrigue. For the moment her energy was gone and she knew it was time to eat again. Since her rescue she had found that returning to normal life was not just a matter of opportunity, of an orderly house, soft sleeping pads and warm covers, cleanliness, many layers of clothing, and ample meals. She could not yet live normally, she needed these things in excess, sometimes eating bowl after bowl of rice, sometimes sleeping the night through and half the morning, bathing again only minutes after she had dressed, requiring Ateki to comb her hair and perfume it three times before she was satisfied. The trouble was, her belief in the reality of the house, the food, the fire in the brazier were interrupted by waking dreams, as if the experience of captivity was so important for her spirit to remember that a deep layer of her mind kept reactivating it. Aoi was patient with this, she believed rationally that, since she was now safe, she should value the insights that her former suffering gave. But it was all too much, she could not plan future cunning while coping with past stress.

The main room of this house was long and narrow and opened to a simple garden. Aoi forced her attention to the outdoors, usually such a refreshing view for the sensitive men and women of the capital. She saw a camellia with fat buds, a young cherry tree bare of leaves, the lily pond and the stone water basin, all wet with rain. To her the glossy leaves, the pattern of branches, the pocked and silvered circle of water surface were not beautiful, had no sentiment or spiritual implications—all that registered was wetness and she leaned around the brazier, spreading her arms to catch more heat.

"The trouble is, lady, we must not delay. People are upset but they will adjust. Let us decide now on a place to begin, one puzzle to solve."

Huddled over the cut slices of charred logs that glowed and whispered with fire deep in the woodgrain yet feeling the chill of rain, Aoi thought she could hear the murmur of guards all speaking the language of the city streets or of the country. "What I wonder," she said, "is why we had that kind of escort. It is the usual thing that a man of high family is asked to take charge, when an important person is to be exiled, and he brings his house guards, young men with some culture in their backgrounds."

"My man had the same question."

"And yet, though the men were not alike, their swords and equipment were all the same. So one person must have outfitted them."

"It is a thread to follow. And I will leave you now. Please rest. Someone will come every morning, if I do not come myself. And there are watchers, so if you need them, we have left a bamboo pole outside each door and if either pole is raised, they will come instantly."

It was what Aoi had been waiting to hear, that help could always be called. She remembered the rough old man who had protected her while seeming to abuse. "That old man—does he still . . . ?" Not wanting to seem to ask for him, she stopped.

"He visits his family. But he is forever apologizing and accusing himself of mistreating you. He begs you to remember him kindly."

"When this is over, the minister will find a place for him, if that is what he prefers, though I think he is like you and enjoys deception."

The Combmaker bowed like a normal person as he left, making Aoi conscious that he must still pity her. She was unreasonably angry that he had not lisped and flopped about as if drunk.

Rain continued into the evening and Aoi could not overcome the feeling that she was out in it, that her robes stuck to her back, that her hair was heavy and clinging. She sat over the brazier but no matter how warm she was in front, she imagined her back to be wet. Finally near tears from the irrationality of it, she had Ateki get out the bed pads and warm the quilt by passing it at a safe distance above the coals of the brazier, and she lay down to sleep. Warmth, when it came, drugged her mind and she sank into sleep as into supporting clouds with a delicious sense of floating security. She slept as if watching herself, as if such bliss of comfort could not be thrown away in an entirely unknowing state.

She heard, with the watching part of her mind, the very discreet rattle of the door latch, heard Ateki leave her small sleeping closet at the front of the house and cross the earth-floored room to the courtyard, heard a bump as the street door opened against the fence, the scrape of wooden clogs removed on the stepping-stone, and then the press, press of heavy feet. This was disturbance and Aoi protested, swung deeper into her pastel clouds, and tried to conceal herself.

"It is a gentleman," said Ateki beside her ear. "I don't know him but he says he is expected."

Aoi swung nearer to her conscious self, prodding understanding but too light and lazy to trouble with speech. She wondered if the minister had come, rescued from his exile and now to be here in hiding with her. Yes, she thought, yes, and pleasure bloomed in her—to know him safe, to speak to him and hear him answer, to have his advice and his physical presence. While Ateki still knelt beside her, the door to the room slid back and a voice said, "Perhaps I am mistaken and you did not expect me, hm?"

Not his voice, she was not to have the minister with her yet. So sharp was her disappointment that she was at once angry, with herself for not knowing what she most wanted, with the man for not being someone else, with the need to come finally in this moment and from now on into reality.

"No, I did not expect you but I should have. After all, this is the way lovers meet, in secret, in the dark of the late night." She sat up and pulled the quilt around her shoulders. "Blow on the coals, Ateki. That will be light enough."

The man was indeed Sukemasa, she could see that now. He came forward bowing and settled himself with hurried grace on a cushion Ateki snatched from a corner. He turned his permanently raised eyebrow toward the maid until Aoi signaled that she should leave them, then when the door had closed, he was at once solicitous, bending forward to pull a corner of the quilt across Aoi's knees, moving the brazier closer, even lifting her hair away from her face to see if she was pleased with his attentions, and then sitting back with his head on one side. "Hm?" he said.

Aoi was testy. "What suits lovers is also appropriate for plotters and spies. No, I am not comfortable because I do not like what we have to do."

"But, lady, you are famous for being quiet and observing what goes on around you. This is no different except that others must be the ones to see, hm?"

"I have never had to hide, it makes me angry, I am not myself." It was so, she knew. She had lost her freedom and with it her usual habits of thought. More than that, anxiety about the minister was preventing her from passing beyond the harsh experiences she had shared with him and she could not live in the reality of the present which seemed to have no meaning because it was easy. Her feelings were confused between grief that she was parted from him, anger that she must keep herself firmly in the moment, just-discovered hate for the person who had conceived the whole plot against them, and realization of power. She had the secret strength of the Combmaker and his invisible helpers in the streets, and at court, this former familiar of the emperor's chambers. "Forgive my temper," she said more gently. "I must thank you for coming after a long day of . . . consulting. What do they say of the emperor's health? Tell me how he is."

"He is perhaps better now that he rests."

"Ah, he rests. He is not frequently brought plans and business, then, by the Minister of the Left, by Genson and his friends who are newly appointed?"

"No."

"And what else do you hear?"

"That an envoy from Silla waits in Kyushu and they cannot decide if they should receive him, that brigands have murdered the governor of Tosa and taken the storehouse and they cannot decide who to send against them, that the governor of Shimosa has protested new taxes, that a large pagoda is to be built at Kohata and the province is to pay for it, that the priests in the mountains are appropriating fields and no one stops them. That the daughter of the Minister of the Left is gathering extra ladies, elaborate clothes, and a new gold-lacquered carriage."

"And who is the new Minister of the Right?"

"That also is not quite decided and the post is still vacant."

"How curious. Why remove one minister if they don't have someone ready to take his place?"

"There are rumors that Akimitsu will have it. Isn't that a scandal, a person no one knows and raised in the country? Of course, I have heard the stories that his father was the old emperor. But can one believe it? He does put himself forward, that one."

"It was Akimitsu who came to warn the minister that they would take him. And it is true about his father."

"Well, he makes himself very officious over there at the office of the minister. They say he has complete control of the promotion list and I can tell you for a fact that able and deserving persons are kept down by that man."

"The minister must depend on him a great deal."

"Too much. He is blind, everyone says so."

"Ah well, this is a time of glory for the Minister of the Left."

Aoi could see how Sukemasa smiled, his eyes shadowed by the light from the low brazier, his mouth one-sided and smug. She felt distaste for his gossip but he had given her a clear picture of conditions in the government in these few minutes.

"I think it might all be too much for that minister, for his abilities, you know, hm? He is not much seen these days. Maybe if there is an important ceremony he will come as he always used to, take the central part, and be solemn in his gorgeous robes. But he does not stay for the banquet, he does not drink with the rest of us now."

"Do you think he is unwell?"

"Please understand that I do not think at all about this little minister. In my position I must worry about the emperor and that is quite enough for me." Aoi noticed, drearily anticipating the complaints that were sure to come, that Sukemasa spoke as if he still attended the emperor.

"So the minister is not enjoying himself. There may be implications here. Find out for me, please, the state of the minister's health."

"Is that all you want me to do? Don't you want to know what they are saying, who meets together, who speaks in angry tones, who is kept waiting by that arrogant and untidy Genson?"

"Such things do not change. What I need to know are unexpected or irrational details, however small. The Minister of the Left has realized his life's ambition and for him not to take full public advantage of his new prominence is unusual and does not make sense. Therefore I need to know more about his reticence."

"Hmpf."

"And there is one other thing, more challenging to your abilities. I must have some papers from the office of the Minister of the Right, any papers that are marked with his seal and are dated within the last two weeks before he was taken away."

Sukemasa was delightedly scandalized. "You want me to go right into the minister's office and take some of his papers? I am eager to serve you, lady, but that office is guarded and only the minister's staff are admitted. Though I do have a friend who is a copier . . . But no, no. It is impossible. A man is flesh and blood and always visible. I cannot make myself into a wraith for invading offices." The very idea made him hum and titter with glee.

"But you are a chamberlain and you are likely to have business anywhere at all in the palace enclosure." Too late she realized her slip.

"A Fifth-Rank Chamberlain, lady, which means honored in retirement. Ah how quickly I would give up this promotion if I could return to the Sixth Rank and attend the emperor's person again. It was a shock, I have not been well these last months. To think how once I longed to change those green trousers of the Sixth Rank, how that obvious mark of inferiority distressed me. Yet I was in the emperor's rooms day and night, right at the center of the world. I dressed his hair, I ordered his robes to be made, received messages. But now I have no position. Actually perhaps I *am* a wraith, a man of no importance, a person others do not desire to see."

"When this is over the minister will remember your help. He is not a man to waste talent and he admires resourcefulness."

"Forgive me, I am in a panic to think of stealing into—"

"You are being modest. I have known many chamberlains and every one of them was capable of stealing into the inner room of the most closely guarded lady."

"But we do not make off with the deeds to the manors! And yet . . . There is a door, I think, in that building that is usually—"

"—locked. Yes, the standard trick. Go in to visit

your friend during the day and unlock it, go back at night and you find it will still be open."

"I see, lady, that chamberlains have no secrets from you." He prepared then to leave, smiling and humming to himself.

"Well, this has been a very intimate talk, lady, though any who thought us lovers would have been surprised to hear us, I think, hm?"

Aoi wanted no innuendos about lovers and she did not answer, which caused Sukemasa to sniff as he moved to leave.

> *"So helpless with words,*
> *I can only play my part*
> *Of the smitten one*
> *And take the poses of love,*
> *Hopelessly mute as you pass.*

"One can at least be a little humorous by quoting bad poetry, lady, hm?"

Aoi laughed then and for the first time began to like him.

Chapter 17

At the minister's house the next morning Lady Omi spoke to O-hana, who had become her serving maid since Aoi's abduction. "It is said that the house is watched. What do you think?"

"I trust the others to know the neighborhood. They say the vendors do not come."

"Because there have been armed men here?"

"Yes, they are afraid of trouble."

O-hana had brought a basin of hot water for washing and she had folded and stored the bed pads, combed out Lady Omi's long hair, given her fresh robes from the rack where they had hung since the night before, and fetched a breakfast tray when the kitchen girl brought it to the door. Now she knelt beside the door panels.

"I have had a message from Lady Aoi and there are some things I must do for her. Perhaps you could open the rain doors and let us see what kind of day we have."

O-hana pushed the latticed door up and hooked it to the ceiling of the verandah, revealing the garden stirred by wind and a sky of lumpy gray clouds, massed low. The rain of the day before had not yet dried and water darkened the paths. "Are the stable men still here or did the guards frighten them off?" Lady Omi asked.

"There are a boy and an old man."

"Do you think the watchers will let me leave?"

"So far no one has been stopped."

"Well, then, we must consult the princess and ask for the use of a carriage, but this is what I am to do and Lady Aoi says you are to go with me—for which I am grateful. She knows I have no talent for deception and you are to give me courage." And Lady Omi explained their errands.

The wicker carriage was light and fast. When the lady and O-hana left the minister's house O-hana had the boy drive the ox quickly. Lady Omi, as was her habit, sat down in the middle of the carriage, well away from the blinds at either end and from the third person who traveled with them. O-hana urged her to the rear and pushed one of her long sleeves out over the back gate so that the several layers of dull-colored and modest cloth would show, arranging the lady's prayer beads to lie on the cloth, as if she were too distracted by the urgency of getting to a temple to notice that they hung there. Anyone watching would see that a woman of low rank traveled out for religious reasons and would assume that she went to pray for the minister.

They spun to a temple nearby and O-hana hurried Lady Omi up the steps, making her awkward in her movements, which, combined with her natural earnestness, made a picture of pious haste. O-hana played her part of maid with distraught mistress, now and then patting and soothing her lady. From the nearby temple they went to one a little farther away and repeated their serious hurrying, returning after an interval of prayer and incense burning. O-hana watched out the rear opening to see if any one person stayed in sight and noticed a man with a wen on his forehead, who had stood leaning against the side of a shop when they stopped the first time and who walked past as they were boarding the carriage outside the second temple. He was dressed in rough clothes and seemed to be a laborer. She saw no man who looked as she imagined a disguised member of the guard would look, though she felt that such followers were in fact there, and so she and Lady Omi continued their precautions.

Next the boy who drove the ox was directed to Kiyomizu Temple. O-hana said the name aloud and piled her lady back into the carriage with as much lack of dignity as she thought permissible. The boy kept his switch busy and the ox, a young brown one, not the stable's best, went so fast that the rocking, groaning basket frame on wheels almost overturned at the first corner. There was a long straight avenue before the tiny streets on the hill leading up to the temple and they would gain time there. Maybe their followers would even drop away, sure where they were bound from the direction they took and from O-hana's deliberate hint. The hill was steep and the ox had to slow to a dragging walk, but at the top they turned as if to let the women off in a side street. Lady Omi drew in her sleeve, the old stable man, who had hidden inside the carriage, took over the boy's job of driving, the boy hid inside, and the carriage became unidentifiable, one among many like it in the crowded streets. They passed slowly now, weaving among carpenters, artisans, priests, boys, women with bundles, all on foot, and occasional small carriages like their own. The old man knew the house. When they had stopped, O-hana looked back to the corner of the street and the man with the wen came in sight and then dropped back.

The ox driver knocked to ask entrance for Lady Omi. Around the house were shops with open fronts, and people stared at the carriage. The gate in the tall board wall opened and the painter himself came to help the women as they stepped to the dismounting stool and onto the roadway.

"I am honored that you visit my poor house, after such a long—" He stopped, realizing that, though he recognized O-hana, he did not know the lady she was urging through the gate. He fell behind to let them walk ahead of him. He was in young middle age, his face a jumble of jutting planes—brows, cheeks, and chin all steeply modeled, mouth sharply edged and flexible. His hair, already graying, stood out at the sides in stiff ragged wings, as if raked from its topknot by frustrated fists. His clothes of home-dyed hemp were rumpled and stained with drops of color.

"I beg you to excuse my rudeness," Lady Omi said, turning herself around to set her feet under her and to catch her breath. "Lady Aoi has asked me to come here." Realizing that Aoi was still thought to be on her way to exile, she gasped and turned to O-hana.

"It was through Lady Aoi, that is," said O-hana, "that this lady knows that you have unusual pigments and colors for painting."

"Yes," breathed Lady Omi. "And that is our errand—to buy paints. And"—she slid her eyes toward O-hana, proud that an invention had occurred to her—"to look at paintings too. For the princess has many times mentioned your skill."

"Ah." All the angles of his face leaped to deeper bases as he smiled. Then he sobered and was for an instant handsome, his face in repose and relieved of its usual excess of expression. "We know, of course, of the trouble . . . in the house of your lady's father," and he bowed before leading them inside.

In spite of the painter's personal untidiness, the one room of his house was immaculately orderly. Paints in small covered stone pots were lined up on his worktable, brushes laid out in a row according to size. There were shelves and bins along one wall, all protected by a hanging of heavy cloth. He picked up the one cushion in the room, which had been set before the worktable, and placed it precisely straight,

motioning for Lady Omi to sit and welcoming
O-hana, who knelt on the floor. "Oi!" he cried, and
his wife put her head through the curtain at the back
of the room, ducking with shyness. Cooking was done
in an earth-floored space behind a hanging of dark
blue cloth. The painter fussed at his desk, clearing
away a scroll panel he had been working on, while his
wife brought slices of persimmon to refresh the
guests.

"And lady," the painter said, his mouth wry, "at a
time like this, the princess has need of pictures?"

"I thought to make her a gift that will console her."

"Tell me what I may show you."

"Actually it is supplies I need."

"Ah, you yourself will paint to ease her distress
about the minister. There is one special color I can
show you. I have been using this beautiful new green
and I have—" He broke off and reached his hand to a
covered shelf.

Unrolling the paper on the floor in front of them, he
set weights at each corner and sat back. It was a scene
of a pond among small hills, a pine tree in the
foreground. Blooming cherry trees grew in the folds of
the landscape and a thatch of tall bamboo swayed on
the bank near the water. As always with this painter,
there were people and a story. A woman sat under the
bamboos gazing at a flower in her hand, and at the
edge of the picture was the figure of a gentleman,
turned in such a way that it was not possible to tell if
he was arriving to meet the lady or leaving her. Green
color shading from palest wash to pine-shadow darkness made the painting glow with light.

"Yes," Lady Omi said, "this green is wonderful."
Emotion made her voice break and she suppressed a
poem about separation.

"It is malachite and copper. But I am still mixing
and experimenting."

"And do you use blue vitriol?"

"Ah, no. That always gave me a milky color and I
abandoned it."

"Then you do not need the blue crystals you ground for paint?"

"I have given them away long ago."

Lady Omi breathed out through her nose to restrain her disappointment.

"Given them away?" O-hana said.

"The dyers use it as a fixative, but even for that it is not so good, they say."

"I see." Lady Omi was now at a loss. The figures in the painting, with so much space between them, so firmly turned from each other, held her attention. "I will have this painting, if I may."

His response was complete stillness as he studied the painting spread on the floor. He turned it and sat again, deciding. Lady Omi, unused to the ways of artists, was troubled. "My problem," the painter said, "is always to decide if it has enough spirit, if the brushwork is sincere." He sighed. The actual problem was that the painter hated to give up his work. Then he was animated again, his face breaking into a jumble of peaks and clefts. "Yes. I will mount it for you. And send it . . . to the minister's house?"

"Yes." O-hana prodded her from behind. "But I need blue vitriol. Can you tell me where to find the dyer?"

"It is not a good color, lady, but if you insist . . ." He escorted them out and they mounted quickly into the carriage while the painter explained to the old man who was driving them the way to the dyer's shop.

That dyer did not use blue vitriol but he sent them on to another shop and when she returned to the minister's mansion at dusk Lady Omi had a cloth full of blue crystals tucked behind her belt, more than would be needed.

When they were ready to start back, O-hana sent the old stable man home on foot and had the boy drive the ox, as he had when they set out. They tried to stop at yet another temple, to complete the day's pretense, but a great procession blocked traffic and they were unable to cross the avenue to get to the the temple beyond. They could see that it was an imperial progress. The emperor was returning to the palace.

Lady Omi did not forget to flourish her prayer beads as the carriage was bumped over the lintel of the gate at the minister's house, ending her role as she had begun it. O-hana saw that the man with the wen was nowhere in sight.

Lady Omi went to her room to study the detailed part of Aoi's note, in which she described exactly how her substitute was to move into the palace and see the emperor every day to touch blue crystals to his eyes. Pretense was over and in this practical matter she felt no uncertainty. She would be concealed by the emperor's faithful chamberlain and she would be comfortable with the application of medicines and bandages, a woman who had had children and a sick husband.

Chapter 18

Early on the second day of her stay in the prince's
secret house, Aoi sent her message to Lady Omi by an
old woman who knocked at the gate and said she was
from the Combmaker. After that, no one came and
Aoi was dull and morose all day, alternately dozing
and fidgeting where she sat in the chilly room, sometimes afraid she would fall into the brazier, sometimes stirring the embers as if that were the only
activity available to her. Her thoughts ran round and
round with worries and imaginings about the minister: Had he survived the boat trip, was he feverish
with infection from his wound, did he ride now
farther to the west, still captive, or was he free and on
his way back to the capital with the men who had
saved him?

When she was restless, as now, she often took out
paper, brush, and inkstone and practiced calligraphy.
The fine gradations of arm movements, the dancing
motion of the brush, the blooms and trails of the ink
as it tracked onto paper in vertical lines calmed her
and promoted order in her thinking. She sat beside

the brazier and littered the floor around her cushion with squares of colored paper on which she had written the oldest and simplest of the traditional folk poems.

> *This forgotten sash*
> *Is all that is left to me,*
> *Still holding his scent.*
> *Can it hold also the tears*
> *That drop at night from my eyes?*
>
> *I stood at the gate*
> *Waving on, though you were gone*
> *From sight into rain*
> *And mist on the farthest hill.*
> *Enemies—that hill, that rain . . .*
>
> *In sorrow I went*
> *To the meadow to lie down*
> *Among tall grasses.*
> *There I hid my weeping eyes,*
> *As once we hid our loving.*

The day was cloudy and dark. She asked for a lamp and wrote on into the dull afternoon, taking one square of paper after the other and wafting them off to the side before beginning again. The longing distilled in the ancient peasant songs she wrote from memory allowed her to gather her own sorrow for the minister and gave her the illogical and comforting notion that if his spirit were no longer in his body it would have come to this house and she would recognize its presence. Such mystical thinking was alien to Aoi but so necessary now that she took it as truth and passed on to pondering the troubles that had resulted in his exile.

The beginning had been the discovery of a young girl's body just under his office, the lewd picture of a blue fish mute accusation. The priest Genson had cast divining bones and foretold revolution and upheaval.

Aoi did not believe in divining bones because she thought they could be manipulated but she believed in priests who grasped, by whatever means they could find, for power. Someone had spread tales about the Minister of the Right: that he had taken Akimitsu's inheritance instead of holding it for him; that he was dissatisfied and ambitious; that he was seen in the company of Taira Munemori, a known pirate and rebel, and therefore must be plotting against the government. The Grand Councillors had been persuaded by all this to abandon their duties and refuse to meet, protesting the minister's pervading influence. The Minister of the Left, who had been happy with an important title and ceremonial and social duties, had suddenly begun issuing edicts, as if he meant to become active in performance of his office. The emperor suffered increasingly from his eye disease and talked of resigning in favor of a weak-minded boy, while Aoi was prevented from treating him by theft of her medicine chest.

The final development had been the arrest and banishment of the minister for disloyalty. The evidence presented was an incriminating letter, everything about it, handwriting and seal, seeming to be authentic. The fact of the letter, bad as it seemed, had given Aoi the clue she needed. Such a letter must be false and must have been manufactured. By whom? Who could have copied the minister's writing and his seal? A clever priest seemed most likely.

What we most need to know, Aoi said in herself to the minister's image, which she would from now on hold in her mind as companion, giving him finally his true emotional presence, is what person has been behind this plot. It is up to me to find the source of so much falseness. Then when the lies are exposed, you can come back. She felt a stir of mental strength, as of a smooth flexing turn, as of power recalled from latency. Ateki served the evening meal and immediately afterward Aoi lay down to sleep, her mind ordered and peaceful. Her dreams were of wide, clear scenes and she moved in them as a woman who succeeds in what she tries to do.

Not used to the bustlings of a small neighborhood, Aoi woke early on the morning of the third day. The next-door housewife was visiting quietly with the tofu seller and their voices carried in the still morning air.

"Cool today," the woman said. "And yet my husband wouldn't wear his padded jacket. He thinks the cold air makes him healthy."

"And him so sick in the summer!"

"Yes, that's why I worry now. Half a block will do today."

"Only half a block? That great son of yours will eat half a block by himself."

"No, no. He's not at home. He went to Lake Biwa to help his uncle, they're building a big house there and taking on extra carpenters. He sends us half his rice chits. We're saving them until we see if his father can keep on working."

The voices sank and then there was the clop of a wooden lid on the tofu tub. They laughed and the woman said, as part of a sentence Aoi could not hear, ". . . evening visitors . . ." Her comfortable tone of voice made Aoi feel that, because the neighborhood seemed to understand the function of this house as a trysting place, she was nestled into an assigned spot, perhaps the object of curiosity but not of censure. She had a sensation of things falling into place, of snick and slide as pieces fitted, of the order and balance of natural arrangement. Secret meetings between men and women were a part of life, and to the woman next door that was not strange or bad or a matter for envy, only something to be noticed. Each house had its feature: this one well-dressed visitors at night, the neighboring one a sick husband. The woman had found a category for the prince's house and settled it into the landscape as a natural element.

Children called, a well wheel creaked, the tofu man sang his way into the distance, "To-o-o-fu, dofu, dof" how about it?" And Aoi lay cozy among quilts with a clear plan for her investigation stretching and stretching step by step toward achieving the minister's return. By the time the Combmaker came to report, she was dressed and ready for him.

He approached her with a certain wariness of eye, looking to see if the temper of two nights ago had changed. When he saw her serious and concentrated, he heaved a great sigh and flopped into the drunken version of his bow.

"Ah, tho. Thith bithineth ith thtarted. It makth me thmile to thtrip the robeth from a prietht and find the bad man inthide."

He leered and rolled his eye to the wall, pulled his soft rags of clothes into several arrangements, changing the shape of his figure each time. As he approached, Aoi could smell wine fumes and wondered if he was really drunk this time. But he dropped his acting and wiped his face wearily. "I had to take a lot of wine last night," he said. "Genson's servants are not fond of him and, once I got them talking, they wanted to drink and complain all night."

"Why don't you go to the kitchen and have some rice before we talk." His tired apology alarmed her, it was so unlike him. He came back with drops of water still gleaming at the edges of his hair from dousing his face. His features were composed and his eyes focused. Satisfaction in his voice, he told her what he had learned of Genson the diviner priest.

"When he casts the bones, every Grand Councillor is invited and so he makes sure that his warnings are immediately known in the government. And the signs are always bad—the time is empty, splitting apart. The minister who is close to the ruler is unyielding in his wrong path. Dragons lurk in the future, water leaks from the well. You know how they talk, these bone casters."

"Um. And what kind of person is he in private?"

"Flies into rages with the servants, then punishes

himself by fasting. There are no women, of course, in the temple, and when he goes out in the streets, he wears a basket hat so he will not see a woman's face. Even his woman relatives—he has two sisters, I believe, and his mother is still living—he will not meet face to face."

"I have heard that he once lectured the prince about women. But the prince is an easy target for such chastising. What of Genson's outside associations?"

"He calls on the other minister and Akimitsu is sometimes about at the temple."

"Does he visit the western city?"

"No, though his carriage is said to go there. The carriage man is rather fat and almost like a crazy man in his devotion to Genson. He goes out in the carriage on mysterious business of his own or of Genson, it might be, and the servants imagine that he does all sorts of outrageous things, saying he buys boys for pages or steals bags of rice and valuables from the temple to sell illegally. The others had to keep quiet until he went to bed. Then it needed very little wine to get these men of Genson's started and they wouldn't stop." He passed his hand over bleary eyes.

"Even his personal servants talked about him? He must make himself unpopular indeed."

"No, these were outside men, from the stables, the carpenters' shop, the kitchen. For personal service he has a young page."

Again Aoi said simply, "Um."

"There were strange murmurs about gold."

"Gold?"

"They wouldn't say straight out but it seems that gold is the favored offering at that temple and they seem to think it doesn't all go to the storehouse."

"Someone steals it? Are you saying that Genson . . .?"

"No, I am not saying that, because they would not say it. But they would make a remark about treasure in the carriage, then they would all laugh or shut someone up by pouring wine in his mouth. The most I can say is that there is something strange at that temple and it has to do with gold."

Aoi looked at him, willing him to explain further, but he shrugged and said no more. She moved to another topic. "What can you tell me about the other minister? Sukemasa says he does not go about."

"I will ask around," he said, but his eye did not light with malice as when he talked of priests. He moved without dramatics to the door and Aoi heard him laughing with Ateki on his way out. Recounting Genson's faults had revived him.

The day's leisure was surprisingly refreshing for Aoi. She rested, she took scrolls from the box O-hana had rescued and browsed among them, she wrote over and over again a line of Chinese poetry that had come into her mind.

> *And will my kind thought warm you in*
> *the cold time?*

The minister was less present in her as she felt her own strength grow and her mind become more and more ordered. Ateki and the woman of the house talked in low voices, sounds of the neighborhood made a web of place that held Aoi in her new identity of lone woman. Somewhere, she knew, the Comb-maker's people watched.

Sukemasa came after dark but not as late as the previous time. With an air of indifference, he put down a roll of papers on the floor before Aoi's knees and would not tell her how he had stolen them, pretending that such feats of stealth were routine for a man of his abilities. Aoi put them aside to examine in sunlight. Sukemasa sucked slightly on his teeth and looked around as if expecting refreshment. He may have been tuned to sounds from the kitchen, for just then Ateki slid open the door panel and advanced into the room on her knees, pushing a tray ahead of her. She offered him small fish broiled on skewers and tiny rice cakes. His eyes widened at the elegance of Ateki's preparation, at garnishes of fresh bamboo leaves and red fish roe. Honored and reassured by these attentions, he became more agreeable as he began to speak.

"I have something to show you that may encourage you. Officially the government believes that the minister is still on his way west, but in the city copies of this are passed about." He handed her a sheet of paper with a drawing on it.

Aoi saw that in general it resembled the fish picture that had been found under the girl's body, so long ago now, it seemed. But the style of the brushwork was not the same, just as crude but done by a different hand. It showed a large fish, washed with blue color, swimming away from hands that grasped after it.

"This may be entirely false but there are rumors and it may be that the city knows better than the ministers," Sukemasa said. He saw that emotion threatened Aoi's composure and chattered on about joy in the shops because, with the help of people like themselves, an unpopular move of the government had been thwarted; and how the avenues were full of jubilant and entirely disrespectful men. Aoi, lightheaded with relief, could not respond and he soon moved on to his own news.

"The other minister, lady, is not ill but he is not well, if you understand me. That is, he is unhappy and stubborn."

He paused to eat from a skewer with elaborate delicacy and would not continue until Aoi prompted him, "Stubborn?"

"Yes. He avoids everyone because they want him to appoint Akimitsu as Minister of the Right and for some reason he won't do it."

"He is not an unprincipled man and perhaps he knows that the removal of the Minister of the Right is suspicious. That is an interesting thought. But in any case he would not care for the idea of Akimitsu in that office. Who is pressing him on this?"

"Akimitsu himself, of course. And the minister won't let him in the house. Genson also calls and is refused. The councillors are all ill, they say, but it is only that they are afraid to take sides, hm?"

"Genson interests me. What do you know of him?"

"Ah." Sukemasa took a folded paper tissue from the breast of his robes and wiped his fingers, head on one side, eyebrow arched high. He did not admire priests and their ascetic denials. "He is fierce in his piety." He nodded, pleased with this summation. "Yes, he is really quite a fierce angry little man. Always correcting people."

Aoi was careful not to smile.

Sukemasa went on. "There are to be new laws, if he continues in his present influence. At least that is what he believes, but he knows nothing of the ways of government. He thinks men will do what they promise."

"New laws?"

"Why, he wants us all to get up at dawn and gather at the district temples to pray. He would dictate our diet—no meat or strong flavors—so that we would eat as priests do. He hates women and would save us from the dangers they lead us into."

"A pious man, angry and righteous. Has he no good qualities?"

"He is famous for calligraphy, people ask him for lines from the sutras to decorate their screens. He is kind to his page."

"Is his kindness so rare that this one instance of the page is remarkable?"

Sukemasa put his hand across his mouth to hide a malicious smile. The eyebrow shot higher. "He quite dotes on this page, so much that the poor boy is almost a prisoner. He keeps him by his side at night and never allows him beyond the temple walls except to accompany himself. But he gives him the finest robes allowed and orders special food for him. People notice, hm?"

"So. Needing affection, he tries to take it by force. It is pitiable and it never works."

Sukemasa, feeling himself chided for lacking sympathy, answered soberly, "You are right. For the boy has run off and Genson has sent his carriage man looking for him everywhere."

"Um. What do you know of Genson's family?"

"Some"—he waved his hand airily to imply people of no consequence—"female relatives are all that are left. His father was a Minister of Civil Affairs but he died young. In fact, Genson was sent into a monastery when he was only a boy—to settle him, you know, because his father was dying. So he has spent practically his whole life . . ." Distaste for such a life clear in the angle of his eyebrow and the downward turn of his mouth, the tilt of his nose, Sukemasa's voice trailed away. He would devote no more energy to explaining Genson.

"What you tell me is very important," Aoi said. "I have as much need of past histories as of present doings. Do you know Akimitsu very well?"

"No." He began preparations to leave, tightening his belts, straightening his posture, arranging his features into formal seriousness, and tilting forward to bow. "No, I don't have much acquaintance with Akimitsu but I know just the person to ask." He smiled, for the first time not affected or mocking. "You are finding it peaceful here, hm? I can see that you rest." He sighed. "If only my beloved emperor could have such benefit from his rest. His eyes are no better, they say." Aoi looked up with keen interest. "Oh, I keep in touch with my friends who are still in service. He suffers. And this situation in the government makes him impatient, but he can do nothing."

She signaled Ateki with a slight tap on the floor, the doors slid open almost silently, and Sukemasa, man about the palace, took his leave.

In another part of the city, a palmleaf carriage, the broad woven strips of its covering ragged around the edges and everywhere stained with water marks and mildew, passed along the avenue among the lacquered and brocade-covered carts of government officials. It was scorned by all who saw it as not only modest but neglected, yet its tall wheels turned rapidly, all its workings solid and quiet, and an aristocrat pulling up from behind in a carriage with crests woven into its brocade cover raised his blind as he went by to admire the plump young ox, black as oil. Tapping his switch along the ribs of the ox, the boy who drove it recognized the calculating look in the man's eye and raised his lip to sneer. "We don't sell oxes," he called and laughed to see the blind snap down as the fine cart drew away.

"No rice tonight," came in a deep growling voice from inside the carriage behind the boy and his face lapsed back into its usual dull lack of expression.

The man inside was in charge of the carriage of the priest Genson and considered himself, the boy, and the carriage to represent his modest and proper master even when he did not travel with them. For important trips the carriage man himself drove the ox. But he was corpulent and no longer young and when there were errands to do, he rode inside, watching the way through the front screen and calling out to the boy directions for turning or stopping. They crossed the main avenue and went for a long while down a wide straight street on the western side of the city. Turning north, they threaded into a busier section, stopping several times to speak to men who hailed the carriage and seemed to know the man inside. Their first stop was beside a house made of warped boards and plastered with mud to close the cracks. A figure wearing a country woman's white headdress came out to speak to the boy, but was summoned by a heavy voice from behind the rear screen. Hearing that, she ducked back into the house and a man appeared, limping on a bandaged leg. An argument developed but then the carriage man could be heard to say, ". . . because I know where you were last night and how you burned your leg," and he laughed. The man limped back into the house and returned with a large wrapped parcel, which he passed to hands that reached out over the rear gate, and the carriage departed.

Next they stopped at a livery stable, where there was a discussion with two men that ended in the turning over of another parcel, this one long and slender, wrapped in cloth. The voice inside called out the next destination to the boy and they drove farther west to a long rambling building with a sagging roof that was a warehouse for a great lord of one of the western provinces. Men were working inside an open door, stacking bags of rice. One of them called that he would fetch the warehouse manager.

There was a period of talk, the fat carriage man laughed and laughed, the provincial lord's man did not join him. The long package wrapped in silk was opened and the scroll inside partly unrolled. The warehouse manager nodded and the scroll was carefully tied up again in its cloth. Then the large bundle that had come from the man with the bandaged leg was lifted down and both were taken into the office of the long building. When the man reappeared after some time he carried a small heavy bag which he gave to the carriage man, turning away almost before the deep, grating voice had finished saying parting words.

The watcher who saw all this, being hungry, left off following the limp-sided carriage and walked to the next street where he could hear a dumpling man calling. Time enough to report later. It was a long way to Sukemasa's house, the wind blew cold, and he needed to fortify himself with hot food.

Chapter 19

The house of the Minister of the Right was changed in its atmosphere from the busy smooth-running home of a high official to a still and echoing collection of rooms and corridors, where the servants spoke in whispers, the blinds rattled in the empty main hall, women wept in corners, curtain frames sat unused and askew, and solemn guards patrolled the grounds. Not a single servant had left but the princess had lost two of her ladies and, though she protested that she found it no hardship, the company of Lady Takumi, with her tendency to wail and lament, and Lady Miyuki, silent and impassive, was not cheering. Only O-hana's sensible persence comforted her.

Darkness came early, now that the Tenth Month advanced, and the heavy rain doors were shut promptly at dusk, making the rooms blacker than the garden. The princess, on this night, went early to bed and sent away her ladies to their own rooms. Lady Takumi could never pass the places where Aoi and Lady Omi had lived without sighs, as Lady Miyuki went into her room and she continued alone down the dark hall.

The princess, though she was not active during the day, wore herself out with worrying and slept heavily at night, distressed by dreams of helplessness. Just before dawn, she sat up blindly, pushing away the bedclothes, confused by a dream of fire. Distant sounds of crackling persisted after her eyes were open, she stood and ran to the door. As she began to slide it back, smoke poured in, blinding her, making her cough. There was no other way out except through the garden, and that way was closed off by the rain doors.

How was it that the maids opened these great panels? Anger, always the first of the princess's emotions, hardened her. She would not be a woman who could not open a door when threatened. Pushing outward, she wondered why the top panel did not move. It should swing up. But of course there must be hooks or bolts. She nearly panicked then, she had never worked a bolt in her life. Her anger told her that any person with sense could do such a simple thing, that she had seen it done a thousand times and she must remember. Feeling along the seam between the halves of the door, she came to knobs and straps. Pushing down did not move them but when she pulled up, they slid and the door, released, groaned a little as a movement of air puffed it outward. The princess stretched herself on the edge of the lower door, forcing the upper half outward, and rolled through the opening. Along the side of the house to her right she could see red light that wavered into the garden, and suddenly burst through the thatch of the roof, racing, leaping, springing up in new places in gay little sprigs of flame. Servants began to scramble from their rooms behind the kitchen, carrying buckets of water. Lady Takumi's voice came high and desperate from the princess's room, where she had run to rescue her. A kitchen maid jumped onto the verandah and held up the door the princess had undone to let her through. Lady Takumi's clothes were black and nearly torn from her sides. She had passed through the fire in the hall to get to her princess and she told them that it was Lady Miyuki's room that burned. By now the fire stood strongly in the whole space of Miyuki's room and not even the bravest of the guards could go in to look for her.

The minister's efficient servants passed buckets of water in teams, but the fire had taken hold and could not be stopped. The whole western wing burned in a holocaust of flame that roared into the dawn sky. By the time full daylight had come, only charred posts and roof framing remained.

Hampered by Lady Takumi's distracted dithering, O-hana was trying to comfort the princess when a maid came to say that one of the stable men wanted to speak to her. He led O-hana through the garden and to a place just outside Miyuki's room, pointing mutely. Pinned to the floor by a short sword through the breast, was the pitiful burned body of Lady Miyuki.

Already distressed almost beyond endurance, the princess shrank away when O-hana told her that Lady Miyuki had died in the fire. In a fit of denial, she retreated behind a curtain, shaking her head, holding up her open hands as if to ward off further news. Lady Takumi wept and wailed, as she always did, and O-hana soon became aware that she was saying the name Akimitsu.

"Poor man! So devoted and she so cold. Now I am glad I did it," said Lady Takumi.

"Pardon me, lady, but what did you do that makes you now glad?" O-hana drew her away from the princess's curtain and spoke quietly.

"She must have been ashamed of her handwriting. Certainly it was not particularly refined and it had an awkward stiffness—she was very stiff herself, so that was not surprising—but still it was not impossible. And yet," she broke off to send a long wail to the rafters, "with all his attentions, she never let him have an answer."

"So we all thought. But you, my lady—"

"I had a poem she had written when the princess assigned us the topic of the spring cuckoo for a competition. I can't think why I kept it, there was a surprising turn of thought in the second part or something. But I gave it to the maid yesterday when she was waiting for an answer to one of those gray notes. Now he will have something to remember her by, but if it hadn't been for me . . ."

O-hana did not comment but she had observed this lady for a long time. Lady Takumi, taking credit to herself for giving comfort to Amikitsu, had in fact sent the poem because she thought Miyuki's handwriting so inferior that Akimitsu would have less respect for her character when he saw it.

The princess called to O-hana from behind the curtain. She had summoned her iron control and she spoke calmly. "Send for the large carriage. We must leave here. I will feel safer in the palace, we can move to my husband's apartment there."

"Yes, I will go at once."

"Lady Takumi," the princess said, "wouldn't you like to visit your home and see your parents? They must be worried about you, with all the bad things that have happened here. There are many ladies at the palace who can take your place and, of course, Lady Omi is already there. I think I can spare you, if you would like to leave for a while." It was a suggestion, made in tactful language, but the princess's tone did not imply that there was any choice. Lady Takumi left to see if she had any clothes that did not smell of smoke.

O-hana, before she began to pack the princess's boxes, went to the kitchen where she knew she would find a young girl of the Combmaker's band. She instructed her carefully: that she should go to the Combmaker and tell him at once of this disaster. She took the girl to the ruined room and showed her the body, so that she could describe it exactly as it lay, pinned by the burned sword. And she made the girl repeat Lady Takumi's words about sending a poem to Akimitsu until she was sure the report Aoi would eventually receive would be accurate.

And so they all left the house of the Minister of the Right. The servants went home to their villages, the garden grew where it would, the unoccupied main hall and east wing became dusty and full of the stale air of an abandoned place. There was no one to order repairs and the west wing remained open to the rain. The old gatekeeper and his sons kept watch and casual thieves were sometimes dragged down from the wall. But the damaged house stood as testament to the minister's fallen fortunes.

Chapter 20

On the morning of the fire at the minister's house, Aoi was up early, anticipating daylight and examination of the seals on the minister's papers. But while the sky was no more than palely lit, the girl came to tell her what had happened. She repeated Lady Takumi's words as she had been made to learn them and she described the body of Lady Miyuki in such vivid and gruesome terms that Aoi closed her ears with her hands and dismissed her, after telling Ateki to give her some fruit.

Before she had time to assess this new horror, another messenger came, this one from the Comb-maker. He was a thin intense boy of about twelve whose eyes appeared huge because of the emaciation of his face. All knobs, his arms stuck out from a dirty robe too small for him. He twiddled nervously, looking from side to side in the closed room, and he had a habit of gripping his elbows to his sides and hunching his shoulders, with the effect of drawing him to the smallest possible physical mass. When he spoke Aoi understood this hiding reflex, for he had a foreign accent.

"He no come—gone—too far."

"I see. I don't mean to burden him to make his way here every day. Tell him to come when there is some reason. I will always be here."

"Unh?"

"Say to him . . . come any time. Not to come . . . fine."

"He say—any need—you have?"

"Unh?"

The boy frowned, looked from side to side, began to stutter. "He s-s-say—tell him—orders."

"No. No orders."

"He say—Did you get message, fire?"

"Yes. Yes, the girl came."

"Good, good."

Not sure he had finished his errand but wanting to get into the open streets again, the boy gripped his fingertips together, snugged his elbows to his ribs, and looked at Aoi, hoping she would release him. Instead she called Ateki and the woman who managed the house, who was so self-effacing that she was never called by name.

"It is customary to reward a messenger. Haven't I seen a box of man's clothes around here?"

Ateki shook her head, she didn't know.

"But you," she said to the woman, "find a robe and give it to him—no, don't just give it to him or he will sell it. Put it on him, and take away that—" There was no word to describe the ragged garment the child wore. "Tie his belts up snugly, let him feel some warmth. And feed him." She turned to the boy. "You come . . . every day . . . we give rice," and she watched him tag behind the woman, who first fetched a robe from a box in the bedding cupboard, distressed that Aoi expected her to betray the prince's trust by giving away one of his possessions. Aoi reassured her. The boy walked with a limp, one foot twisted strongly inward.

This encounter, coming while the story of the fire still shuddered uncomprehended at the back of Aoi's mind, set the tone for a cold gray day. Such a child, son of immigrants from somewhere on the mainland, who were always suspect and unpopular, would have been shunned all his life and now must be orphaned or abandoned. With his inadquate language and his physical deformity, employment would be impossible, and even living in the streets as he did would be harder for him than for a child with less difference to pay for. The child's condition was one more sad reality in the fabric of a world of punishments. She began to worry that he would not let her do the small charity of giving him food and clothes and she wondered what threat she could use to force him, to make him let her help. Ah Aoi, she said in herself, this is pride. You should not order the lives of others, even for their own good. Yes, she answered herself, if I were to see this boy as my carriage passed, I would take no notice. But when he sits on my floor and shakes in thin clothes, he is given to me as one person and I must try. But not by force, said the other self. Trust the gods. If you are to help this child, he will come.

On this day the Tenth Month declared its character. Clouds of leaden gray had massed low and a steady wind blew between the houses, trailing the bamboo leaves to one side, riffling the water in the garden's fish pond, moaning through the eaves and under the floor. Nevertheless, Aoi had the rain doors opened. Strong cold light was good for the fine examining she must do. It was to compare seals that Aoi had asked Sukemasa to bring some of the minister's recent papers. She had in her box a deed to rice fields that she had been given during her service to his daughter and she wanted to compare that seal with those of more recently marked documents.

The minister's seal was a square one, the stylized letters which represented his name intricately woven together within a narrow border. The value of seals was that each one had small individualities from the

she should admit him, control of her voice was not yet sure when the door panel slid back, revealing him bowing in the hall, a stranger behind him. She understood his greeting, his explanation that his companion was (someone) of (some) Province and that he had known Akimitsu when he was a boy. But her mind would not focus, she could not grasp details. Desperately she tapped the floor and Ateki brought hot tofu dressed with spiced bean paste and a small kettle of warmed wine. During the serving, tasting, and compliments she wrenched her thoughts toward the visitors. Even so the stranger—what *was* his name?—was well into his story before Aoi really understood his words.

"—tormented him from the moment he arrived. He was girlish, you see, raised in that house by women. Your could hardly blame the boys, his speech was so formal and womanish it was almost impossible to understand him. 'Would you do me the kind favor . . . ' he would say, even to those boys the same age or younger. Boys have no mercy in them. They put burs under his saddle when the lord made him learn to ride, they ducked him in the horse trough." The man laughed, apologizing. "Yes, I know. Unkind. But he was such a . . . Well, he was like a willow and those boys were oaks."

Aoi could only murmur sympathy. Sukemasa sucked his teeth and leaned over to choose another cube of tofu, absorbed but clucking on cue when he caught Aoi's eye. "Terrible. Boys, hm?"

"He found a way, though. There was a teacher and every morning the boys had school. They had to be caught, sometimes, and driven to their writing desks. But there he mastered them."

"Forgive me, but how . . ."

"Sorry, I thought I explained," said Sukemasa. "This gentleman"—he did not say the name and in fact Aoi never learned it—"was at that time steward on the estate."

"Yes, Akimitsu knew all the old poems, he handled the brush with skill. Sometimes he would imitate the writing of the older boy, who was his special tormentor, and write scandalous things about the teacher, leaving the paper on the floor for him to find."

"Such tricks are the special trial of teachers," Aoi said. "My father was always impatient with them, and his students were princes."

"Ah, that was another thing," said the man. "This business of being a prince. At first he would throw it in their faces but it enraged the boys so that he soon let it drop. For friends he turned to the farmer's sons and they became a very mischievous band. Especially when they got older."

"Girls?" said Sukemasa.

The gentleman nodded his head. "There were tales, stories very much . . . not nice."

"But the lord, he must have tried to . . ." said Aoi.

"Yes. And it would work for a while. He is a very strong man, that lord—actually, physically, I mean. He rides all day—or did then, when he was young— he throws rice sheaves on the rack as fast as his youngest farmers can. I've seen him leap the barrier and wrestle two men at once, to keep them from running away from the manor. The boy admired him and if he was threatened or scolded by the lord, he would be meek and not look up for a week."

"He left when he married, I suppose?" said Sukemasa, licking his fingertips, looking about for wine, which Ateki had set a little beyond his reach. Aoi poured for him and offered more to the gentleman, who had been required to talk so much that his original cup was still full. He drank, accepted the refill, and continued his story.

"Yes, he married. But he left before that."

"Oh?"

"Things disappeared from the storehouse. The count of rice bags would come up short, bolts of cloth disappeared. I would be questioned and show the receipts but the lord would say there was something odd about them or that he did not remember issuing them. I suspected Akimitsu but I never said so."

The man did not explain but his glance invited Aoi to imagine the pitfalls of accusation in such a case. Sukemasa nodded, halting the progress of his wine cup. Chamberlains understood the necessity of tact but Aoi had not thought that in the provinces sensibilities were so finely tuned. "And so he left?" she said.

"The lord gave him a small manor and he left to become a lord himself."

"He had manors of his own, if he had only known it," said Aoi.

"He knew. And the lord knew. But it was worth the loss of a few fields to get him off the lord's land. He had caused a lot of trouble and it only grew worse as he came to maturity."

"So he took land he didn't need," said Aoi.

"Um," said the gentleman, considering his reply. Former country life still showed in sun-darkened skin, now loose around his mouth, and a skeptical cut of the eye as he said, "So do'm all," a folk expression. He ducked his head in apology but looked to Aoi and Sukemasa for agreement.

Sukemasa, used to managing visits, their beginnings and their ends, set his hands on his knees with decision, bundled the gentleman from the room amid thanks from Aoi, and was soon out the door with easy dispatch. Only to return and lean for a moment around the half-closed panel in Ateki's hand. "The other minister," he said.

"Yes?"

"He is ill, so ill that the ceremony installing Akimitsu is postponed."

"Really? But Akimitsu is appointed?"

"Oh yes. There was never any real question. But without the Minister of the Left . . ."

"I see."

A fleeting smile of derision and complicity and he was gone again.

Chapter 21

Sukemasa lived in a modest house that was perfect in every detail. The street wall was white with fresh plaster and the side fences of bamboo were closely bound for privacy from the neighbors. His blinds were hung new every year and retained their green color well past the summer, their edges bound in a brocade woven of black and dark green, their tassels full and rich and never matted with wet from the rain. Colors were sober, giving his rooms a distinction that only those who had seen the gaudy display of other minor officials could appreciate. His one folding screen was a collage of gorgeous dark papers, with a single line of calligraphy in gold, which Sukemasa had written himself. Cushions and bedding were covered with pure white rep, a cloth made on one of his father's estates. The floor gleamed, the bronze of the brazier glowed with subdued luster, a single curtain frame was hung with the same white cloth and decorated with ribbons of deep jasmine yellow, the only bright color in the room. Absolute cleanliness and absolute order were required at all times.

On the night after Sukemasa had taken the former steward to visit Aoi, he lay asleep in this immaculate house, his next day's robes hung on a stand and moving as currents of air stirred through cracks under the rain doors. Cooks and maids slept in their own house beyond the vegetable gardens at the back of the lot, the gate was bolted, the whole property snug and secure. Wind thrashed through the shrubs and bent the trees.

No one saw the single figure that tumbled over the wall and rolled on the ground under a pine tree, boosted too strongly from the other side. His cough of breath as he fell did not carry into the still blackness of any interior, his silent movements around the verandah made no scrapings or knocks. Testing every door, he tried to get inside but could not. So he piled his oil-soaked rags against the rain door of the west side of the house and, hoping that Sukemasa would escape through the main entrance and give access to his famous collection of jade, touched red-hot coals to the pile. Fire bloomed, briefly faded under black smoke, then blazed and gradually climbed along the fitted wood of the doors and into the roof, tearing tissues of flame that faded and streamed as the wind moved, catching at once on several places in the thatch, chunks of burning sedge blowing to the roof of the outbuilding.

When Sukemasa woke, he was facing a wall of flames. He leaped up, terrified, and ran to the opposite doors, but the fire surged into the room behind him. The cords that held the blind burned through and it dropped in front of the burning doors, flame racing among the dry strips and sizzling like firecrackers. In his panic Sukemasa could not make his fingers undo the locks of the entrance door. Wrapping himself in a thick bed pad, he plunged through the section of rain door that was burned through, ribs of glowing red bamboo falling about him from the blind, so that he emerged in a cloud of sparks. The clay of the path was cool to his bare feet, the pad was on fire but not his clothes. Sure that the garden was crowded with murderous arsonists, never looking behind him, pierced by alarm and picking his feet high, his loosened robes streaming behind him, he ran down the back street in the gray light of dawn.

On that same night but long before the dawn, the Combmaker had lifted his face from the dirt of a street in an eastern section of the city, at the end of a mission that had begun the afternoon before when Akimitsu left the palace enclosure by the Sen'yo Gate. The secretary had walked with a purposeful stride, his long full trousers billowing but the sleeves of his robes pulled close to his wrists as he held his hands together. Others passed him, their hands also clasped across their middles and holding erect the ivory shafts that signified their office and the legitimacy of their presence within the palace walls. Mere secretaries were not given such signs of authority but no man so lowered himself as to walk with his arms swinging. The guards looked at the clasped hands, registering respect or disdain according to what they held or what they lacked.

All who passed him recognized the secretary of the Minister of the Left and all were prepared to greet him. They watched with frequent glances to see if he would acknowledge them—he was not a man one could ignore—but Akimitsu moved steadily forward, eyes front, brow tight with concentration. It was his usual way. On the rare occasions when he did absently tip his head toward someone, the man so honored could not be sure if such a salute meant that he was favored or that he should examine his recent past for disrespect or misdeameanor.

Still striding, Akimitsu turned right and walked to the spot against the east wall where his carriage waited each evening. The ox was a slow brown one, the carriage covered in sober gray woven with small designs of the imperial crests he was allowed to display because he was son of an emperor. One man waited with the ox driver, helped him to a seat inside, and mounted his horse to ride ahead and clear the way through the crowded streets. They drove to the Second Ward, to an avenue lined with well-kept walls and massively roofed gates. His own gate, though, where they turned in, was gray with weathering, the pillars cracked, the roofing sedge crumbling and uneven, in places mossy. The ox was unyoked and led away to stables in the rear, the horse rider following. Two servants in untidy livery pulled the carriage by its shafts across the courtyard, turned it, lowered the rear gate, and bumped with several adjustments until the back opening met exactly the floor of the gallery. He stepped out. A maid ran to meet him.

"Can't you learn to do the simplest thing?" Akimitsu said to the men who had pulled the carriage. "Every time I come here I am bruised and knocked about by your clumsiness." And to the bowing maid, "Get out of my way." He kicked at her as he passed and in her fright she fell onto the gallery railing, a very young girl whose mouth gaped. She was pregnant. The thump of angry heels disappeared into the house.

The Combmaker, who had followed him and was now begging in the street outside the gate, considered. It would be easy to go over the wall there where the trumpet vine hung down. The sun was setting, the garden was brushy and full of weeds, and he knew that he would be able to get close enough to the main hall to hear the conversation between Akimitsu and his wife. But because this was not the first time he had followed Akimitsu, he could predict that there would be abuse and weeping, and he had not the stomach for that just now. The vine, though, would serve to hide him, if he sat just beside the mass of slender branches, and he waited.

Akimitsu left on horseback, plunging through the gate, already cantering, scattering pedestrians. The Combmaker drifted along behind him. After a few blocks, the horse was pulled up to a sedate pace, the rider sat erect and alert, looking about, bowing to acquaintances, sober-faced, careful of his way though aloof as he watched those on foot. He rode to the Sixth Ward where his new house was.

Here the gate was broad and impressive, guarded by young men who bowed and took his horse, remarking with easy formality on the cool weather, their master's probable tiredness, and the horse's need for brushing. Akimitsu answered as easily, glanced about the orderly courtyard, and climbed the steps to the gallery. Three ladies dressed in silk robes of autumn colors surrounded him there and walked with him into the house, telling him how they had waited for his arrival, laughing behind their fans at their own tales of listlessness and boredom when he was not with them, saying that they would be utterly crushed when he brought his new wife. He walked within their fluttering colors, smiling at their compliments, directing his eyes behind their fans, observing powdered cheeks, demure eyelids, smoothly flowing black hair, deciding which one he would favor this night.

The Combmaker passed the massive front gate and turned the corner toward the kitchen gate, where he spoke to a middle-aged maid who came out to dip water from the bucket that sat on the edge of the well.

"Ah, I disturb you at a busy time," he said.

"You certainly do. Don't come in here when the master has just arrived. Go! Go away!"

"But it's about autumn mushrooms."

"Unh?"

"I know where there are many. But you must say first that you will take them. Then they will be only an hour old when I deliver them. No one else in the city will have such fresh ones and your cook can say that to your master."

The maid knew her master's taste for outdoing others. She eyed the filthy rags that draped the man in front of her. He stood upright and faced her honestly but just as she was about to decide, one of his eyes slid to an angle, the mouth loosened and she began to have doubts. "Wait," she said. "Let me ask the cook," and she turned back into the house. When she came out again to order mushrooms, the man was gone. "Ran off. I thought there was something funny about him," she muttered to herself and returned to her duties with wine and china cups.

The Combmaker, drawing a dark length of cloth from around his waist and across his head, had made himself a shadow among shadows in the darkening garden and now sat just under the gallery outside the main hall. To his disgust he heard only pleasantries between Akimitsu and the three ladies but he stayed on, now and then flexing his limbs in the damp cold, marveling at the invention and elaboration of romantic banter that came to his ears. Then when two of the ladies retired he thought that Akimitsu's character as it had come out at the old mansion would emerge and he wondered that any woman would voluntarily submit to him. Again he was surprised, hearing only tenderness and soft sighing from the room where Akimitsu and his lady lay together on silk bed pads and under silk quilts within a curtained platform. They seemed to fall asleep.

That's enough for tonight, the Combmaker thought and he took a run at the wall in a deserted corner, hefting himself up and over and dropping into the street. Stiff and chilled, he started home through the dark streets. His way took him along the wall and northward toward the market, where he lived in a hovel against the back of someone else's new shop on the site of his old one. He pulled his lengths of cloth close about his head and edged into the wind with one shoulder forward. Just ahead of him, a man's form appeared as if suddenly materialized from the air and stood facing the wall, making small movements with his hands held high. The Combmaker slumped against the wall and watched. The man ahead of him was securing something above his head. He finished and walked away toward the north. When the Combmaker, following, came to the place where the man had been, he found a small gate and, feeling with his hands, a latchstring attached to a peg concealed in the doorway.

Funny thing, he said to himself. The servants have a way of sneaking out at night. From habit, he followed inconspicuously—he was going in the same direction anyway. The man ahead must be a porter because he wore the wrapped pants and tightly tied waist cloths of those who carried heavy bags of rice or other freight on their backs. But why had he come out so secretly in the late night? And wasn't there something familiar about those shoulders, made so broad by the compression about the waist? The shoulders swayed, the arms bent and swung elbow up and the man ahead of him was trotting. He turned east and the Comb-maker ran to keep him in sight.

Into smaller and smaller streets the Combmaker followed. Here the houses were poor, some with shuttered shop openings. The man stopped at a wooden gate, whistled two notes, and disappeared inside. The Combmaker, when not running to catch up, had for some time been pretending to be drunk, stumbling about with loose knees but always silently. More drunkenly than ever, he now lurched against the same closed gate and pushed. The latch inside gave way with a crack and he was in a tiny courtyard.

A voice inside the house stopped in mid-sentence and the entrance door slid back. "Someone came in," the voice said and in the dark corner where he had let himself fall the Combmaker shook his head in disbelief because he knew that voice. Two figures stood in the faint light from inside the house: the porter he had followed and another, a large heavy-limbed man. The porter saw him, rushed to the corner, and kicked.

"Ish," the Combmaker said.

"Thief!" came back at him in a hissing voice, and then, "Ugh," said the other, dropping the handfuls of rags by which he had dragged him to his feet. "Get on, you can't come in here."

"Thith my houthe. Where'th my wife?" And seeming to comprehend something, "Hah-h-h! Tho! You come in here when I'm gone! Thneaking into my bed—"

The porter smiled as he pushed the Combmaker in the chest so that he fell again. He did not restrain his voice as he said to the large man, "Throw him out." No other person came from the house to see what the disturbance was and the Combmaker decided that there were only these two. The large man advanced, opening his mouth and emitting a hollow sound, just the sound the Combmaker had once heard from a man who was dumb because his tongue had been cut out.

The porter had already gone back inside. The large man was strong and the Combmaker landed on his face in the street and lay there smiling.

Later in the morning he came to report to Aoi. He had heard of the fire at Sukemasa's house and had talked to the servants, who had seen their master burst through the door and run away without warning them that their roof was on fire. They knew him well and were not surprised, but they were so disgusted that they had all gone back to their families and would ask their estate manager to give them other duties.

"And Sukemasa, he is not injured?" Aoi said.

"No one knows. But from the way he ran . . ."

"This makes me think they must know of his association with me."

"If Sukemasa too accounts for the fire in that way, we may never see him here again. He is not a brave one. But there are fires and thefts everywhere, there is no reason to think he is suspected."

"I am so afraid of bringing harm to others from these vicious people. The painter, for instance, to whom I sent Lady Omi. Has his house . . .?"

"No, we have not heard of any accident to the painter. Though I know that a man was found injured just by his fence. Someone had stuck a dead fish into the back of his coat, a strange thing." He sat impassive.

Aoi had not heard before of any direct violence done by the Combmaker's men but she could not find disapproval in herself, only gratitude that the painter's house had not burned. "It seems that your men are the only protection we have, those of us who support the minister. I have never remembered to thank you for the guard who followed Lady Omi and O-hana that day."

"Guard?"

"Yes, in the letter she wrote me afterward, Lady Omi said that O-hana had spotted a man with a wen on his head. They thought he was one of your men, looking out for them."

"I don't have a man like that, and anyway I would never set such a noticeable person to follow somebody."

"So he was not your man. But it is certain, she writes, that he was seen several times during that trip in the carriage. Someone hired him, some person with a connection in the western city, where such men are to be found. You say Genson never goes there. But Akimitsu?"

"Ah." Aoi had brought the conversation to the subject most vivid in his mind and the Combmaker settled his knees more widely and drew his shoulders down as his thoughts arranged themselves. "Today I can tell you a lot about Akimitsu. We have been following him for some time and last night I learned something new. But as much as he moves about—and he seems to live in several places—I don't think he goes beyond the avenue to the west."

"You make mysteries. And if you begin to loll and lisp I won't talk to you." For his bad eye had wandered and she could see that he meant to joke.

"But," he said, "going behind a man when he thinks he is unnoticed requires a little laughing. Else wouldn't I feel myself an arrow strung to the bow?"

"Secret following could cause great harm, it is true. And I agree that we should restrain our arrows until we are sure whom we hunt. But tell me now about Akimitsu's several residences."

"He has first the old house you know of—the one from his grandmother. His wife lives there, though if her father hadn't died two years ago I'm sure she would still live in her old home. The mansion of the former retired empress is a dark old place and it is not kept up, very gloomy and sad. He visits. But then there is the new mansion. It is all finished and takes up half a city block."

"I had no idea it was so grand."

"Yes, it is a large place and there is every luxury inside. Many people are surprised. He keeps his clothes there, and it is where he goes at the end of the day. He sleeps there too. Sometimes."

"There is yet another place?"

"Oh, yes. This man—he is a little like me. He splits himself."

"Oh?"

"Strange. It's something you can see, how he changes his walk, his voice. But I think he doesn't know it."

"You yourself maybe didn't know it at first."

"Unh." The Combmaker was not speculative in that way. "Well, so. He changes houses. At the old mansion he is quite a nasty person." The Combmaker threw out his elbows, puffed up his chest, and scowled to demonstrate. "Then he goes to the new one and he is all . . ." He composed his features and looked composedly from side to side in a benign manner.

"Who lives there with him?"

"There are servants and fine women to attend him. He will probably bring a new wife, they say." He began to laugh again, holding up his hand to show Aoi that he would not let himself slip too far. "And then," he said, "there is the *other* other house."

"Two other houses besides the old mansion?"

"He goes to a very small house in a crowded section

just north of here, a *very* small house. This house is so
poor that it backs up to the house of a porter in the
next street, with a common wall between. He goes
there in the night."

"And who else . . .?"

"No women, only a manservant, a great tall heavy
man who is mute." This was his greatest surprise and
caused him the greatest amusement.

"I am astonished," said Aoi. "What is his manner
in this house?"

"There he is . . ." He flexed his arms and seemed to
grow larger. When he spoke again his voice deepened.
"He wears work garments." Then he lifted his puzzled face to her. "Can you believe I see all that?
Maybe I imagine."

"No, you have instincts. Have you followed the
manservant?"

"Not yet, but we will. One more thing. Genson has
made a trip to the western city."

"What would make him take that risk everyone is
so afraid of?"

"We don't know yet. He went into a house and
stayed for a long time. It was getting dark and the
carriage guards were nervous, they said. He had never
gone there before."

"Is his young page still missing?"

"Yes, he has sent them looking for him. But those
inner servants and pages, you know, they sometimes
come from over there . . ." Aoi did know. Entering
the priesthood, if they were bright enough and could
get in, was a way out of poverty. "And it doesn't do to
ask questions in those rough streets."

"Would he have gone there himself, then, to that
house, looking for his missing page?"

"It is possible. The regular carriage man knew the
place exactly."

Aoi noticed that when it was strange acts of a priest
he talked of, the Combmaker became much sharper
about the face and less amused. He departed soberly,
promising to continue following these two men.

Aoi's only release from the confinement of the house was to walk in the garden. To turn about in the garden more properly expressed the possibilities for movement there. On stone paving between the pine tree and the pond the space was too small for more than a few steps. The wind had stilled and the air was not so much cloudy as thick and white, just on the edge of fog. She wrapped herself in a padded jacket and paced, sometimes watching the circlings of the carp, which seemed to parallel too aptly her own path in this tiny place.

Thoughts of other, larger gardens took her too near the morning's vision of the minister and for a while she erased all images. Until a triple figure of Akimitsu intruded, walking out of his past: the angry one, resentful toward women; the good one, applying for membership in the world of grown men; and the leader of farm boys. For a long time Aoi walked step and step, pondering the three houses of Akimitsu.

Chapter 22

When this is over, Aoi thought, I will have had quite enough of solitude. For two days it rained. The house, which for Aoi meant a single room, was dusky even at noontime. Ateki and the woman had their tasks and their shopping, which made Aoi so jealous that she began to resent their companionship with each other, as if it were a conspiracy to emphasize her loneliness. The Combmaker did not come, though the lame boy brought apologies and strayed eagerly into the kitchen at the end of his fractured sentences to Aoi. Sukemasa would probably never return from his father's place in the country, once he had pondered the cowardice of his abandonment of his servants in the flight from the burning house.

She had plenty of time to think, of course. But her isolation led her to pity more than to sharp analysis— pity for the child Genson, given to the priests before he was old enough to know what that life was; pity for the child Akimitsu, smothered in an old woman's mansion. But pity did not prevent her from developing ledgers under each child's image, accounts of the deposit of traits needed for these crimes against the minister. She felt that when credit swelled on one side or the other, she would take action. As the dreary hours passed, she knew that she waited only for a final tip of the balance.

And then in the early evening of the second day, she heard Ateki go to the street door. The visitor came behind her to the main room. It was Sukemasa.

"Forgive me for neglecting you these past few days. I have been in the country visiting my father." His face haughtier than ever, he seemed to intend to offer no reason for the trip.

Aoi faced him kindly. "I have heard that your house was destroyed. Such a pity. They say the fire took everything in it."

"Unh. My jade, though, was in a stone storeroom and should be unharmed. I don't think it is safe to go back just yet, those people may still be around. It was pure animosity, personal to me." A spasm of contraction crossed his features but Aoi could not tell if he expressed fright, outrage, denial, or excusing explanation, in case she had heard that he ran away in a panic.

"And so, naturally, you went to your father's house." She would make it easy for him, not requiring him to explain how he had reached the country. Probably he had bribed a farmer with one of his robes to take him there instead of going to market. "He will have been pleased to see you."

From Sukemasa's alarmed expression, she doubted that his father's reception had been generous. But then his face cleared and he said cheerfully, "I have never been one for bravery, the least thing unexpected and I take flight, hm?"

"I see." Aoi was so bemused by this admission that she could not think how to go on. If he had been in the country, surely he had nothing to tell her about Genson or Akimitsu.

"Actually, it is a fortunate thing I went there. Because my father used to know Akimitsu."

Aoi's startled interest encouraged him. He smiled his downturned smile, his scarred eyebrow stretched higher, he sucked his teeth and looked around absently at the bare floor, as if to discover where he had left his wine and tidbits. Ateki must be still preparing them but to reassure him, Aoi tapped the floor. Sukemasa took a tissue of paper from his robe and wiped his brow, opening his mouth as if to clear a dry throat. When he heard Ateki's steps in the hall, he began to relate what his father knew of Akimitsu.

"You see, he married the daughter of my father's friend, a man who served with Father in the provincial government. When Akimitsu came to Harima Province where that friend lives, he had only a small estate of four farms and a poor village, which a lord in Tamba, who was his guardian, had given him. But he had a way with the farmers and he taxed them lightly so that they produced well for him yet had enough for themselves. Soon the neighboring farmers wanted their lands joined to his, but they were assigned to one of the estates that belonged to Father's friend. So Akimitsu began to call on this provincial official and he got a glimpse of a young daughter—very young, quite beautiful, they say." He paused to consider. "Beautiful as the young often are, just because they are young." There was wistfulness in his eyes. His own youth, when he had been so happy serving the emperor, was gone and the loss of his house had further wiped out that time. Aoi witheld her sympathy. Sukemasa would always find some reason to make himself proud. "So they gave her to him," he continued, "and the neighboring estate, too. A lovely young girl who was always called Miyuki."

It was not the shock it might have been because Aoi knew that Miyuki's home had been in Harima Province. "But what became of her?" she said. "His present wife is a highborn woman of the capital." Loyalty to Miyuki's memory kept her from telling him that Akimitsu had recently been courting his former wife without realizing who she was and she had to force attention to Sukemasa's words and found she caught only a few of them.

". . . moved her into his own house . . . soon developed interests nearer to the capital . . . took over his inherited estates . . . some said he raided to increase his holdings."

Miyuki: standing in the splayed light of a bamboo blind, her face glowing with wonderment at the little carved sheep, waked to full mobile expression by the art of a Chinese carver. Suddenly Aoi wanted that sheep, no matter how blackened. "And so," she said, "he neglected his beautiful young wife in Harima Province and eventually abandoned her."

Sukemasa accepted this analysis casually. "After he left, she became ill," he said, sipping wine. "For years she would not speak. Perhaps she still sits in her father's house, silent as a stone." Had Sukemasa's father used the same apt image, recalling a phrase used by his friend in speaking of his daughter? Sukemasa had no appreciation of the drama of this poor forgotten wife. Aoi was overcome with bitterness. She sipped her own wine, joining Sukemasa for the first time in his indulgences. It gave her an excuse to be silent.

Sukemasa was picking among an assortment of cold grilled vegetables sprinkled with sesame seeds, intent on his choosing. "The other minister's illness advances. Three Grand Councillors have called on him to speak for Akimitsu but he would not see them. He spends his days behind a curtain."

"How do you know these things?"

"Oh, you cannot imagine the stir about all this, hm? One's friends talk of nothing else, one's servants know every detail. It is no great trick to find out even what he refuses to eat." Sukemasa was not refusing anything. His chopsticks were busy and he finished all the vegetables. "Why, Genson himself cannot get in to see him, though he calls every hour."

"I see," said Aoi.

That night there was a fire several blocks north of

the prince's house, a fire of such extent that early
risers in Aoi's neighborhood saw the smoke and
flames and she was wakened by their exclamations.
Many ran to help and there was a distant hubbub of
shouts and orders. Carriages plunged through the
streets and people ran in both directions, mothers
crying after their children not to get in the way. Men
pounded on closed shutters to wake their friends,
women shouted after them that they should keep their
eyes open, meaning that they should loot if they
could. Dawn wind rose, carrying sparks eastward. In
the end forty houses burned.

The origin of the fire had been in the other minister's compound and it had developed into a fierce
blaze in the main building before it was discovered.
The woman of the prince's house went out and soon
brought the dismal news that the Minister of the Left
and one of her women had died when the roof
collapsed. The other minister, nearly demented, had
been taken to safety in the palace enclosure, his wife
had fallen down in a faint and the doctors could not
revive her. Aoi's impulse was to go to the palace to see
if she could help. She had known the wife of this
minister for a long time, though because of Aoi's
duties with the princess, they had not had much
contact lately. Yet, involved on the other side in the
minister's exile and required to keep her presence in
the capital a secret, she could not present herself to
the minister and his family.

All morning crowds gathered at the open walls of
shops, children ran in excited packs, men passed back
into the neighborhood, talking in outdoor voices,
telling each other what they had seen, what they had
done to help, who had ordered them about with heavy
authority, what they had broken or stolen in revenge.
The prince's woman servant became nervous because
this house was known to belong to a nobleman. She
made rounds, checking that every rain door was
latched. When she heard the call, "Pity, pity!" she
would not go to the gate to see who asked for food.

Ateki argued with her and the discussion carried to Aoi's place in the main room.

"It will be a priest and it is a sin to refuse him, my mother always taught me that," said Ateki's young voice.

"You have not been out," said the woman. "People are loud out there, they swing their elbows, knocking aside any who get in their way. They are glad to see the minister lose his house."

"But such hatefulness has nothing to do with us."

"You are wrong. They know there is no man here. I will not open that gate."

"But it is only a begging priest." And Ateki stepped into her shoes and crossed the few stones to the gate, the woman groaning at her folly.

"You see, it is only a poor priest," Ateki was heard to say. "I will just ask you, sir, to give me your bowl and if you'll wait right there, I will soon return." Her wooden house clogs clopped on the earth floor as she crossed to the pot hanging over the kitchen fire.

"Careful, careful!" the woman cried and there was a thump.

"Ah, he's ill," said Ateki. "He needs food. I'll just . . ."

Aoi rose and went down the hall toward the steps that descended to the earth-floored room. A man in dirty white clothes lay toppled over at the edge of the hall floor, his basket hat dislodged and upside down. Wrappings of white cloth obscured his face. As she approached, Aoi saw that his eyes opened to slits and he watched her skirts come nearer. She backed away instinctively and hesitated. If he was a priest weak from hunger, his attention would be toward Ateki and the cooking pot. Yet if he was ill and needed attention . . . ? While she balanced caution and obligation, the man moved slightly, drawing his arms in from their outflung position and tensing in almost imperceptible ways. Aoi continued to step backward.

The woman, too, watched him and suddenly she moved, darting out the door to the front courtyard.

Ateki was cooing about the rich broth she ladled into his begging bowl, reciting that she was adding three squares of tofu, a piece of fried fish, a slice of onion, spinach leaves, and that she would break a fresh egg into it. The man's eyes closed, he rolled his head on the floor and thought that Aoi would not see that he raised his lids again and looked toward the door. The woman, who had been so alarmed just a minute before because someone was allowed to enter, was now holding the gate ajar. A burly arm and shoulder in beggar's rags thrust in, a rough voice spoke, "You put up that there pole. Trouble? That priest, is it?"

"I told her not to—" the woman said.

"You!" he shouted toward the priest. Stout bulk filling the gateway made mockery of his costume of beggar. Legs round as pillars, a tight tub of belly, swelling forearms were topped by a ball-shaped head rimmed with black curls bound in a clumsy topknot. His smile as he advanced was clearly because he expected exercise.

Ateki, still detailing the wealth of her stew, unaware that the door had opened to admit another man, came between the beggar and the priest, who was just reviving and sitting up on the bottom step. With her back turned, Ateki did not see the beggar but she saw Aoi frozen with indecision in the hall and she stopped in confusion. Too quickly for her, the priest snatched the bowl, tossed hot liquid into the beggar's face, and darted past as the huge man doubled over to wipe his eyes on the ragged hem of his clothes. The gate bounced and rattled as the priest ran into the street.

The beggar ran after him but soon returned, bereaved, opening and closing his huge fists and heaving great breaths. "That one!" he roared. "Fool, fool! Puts on them whites, them hat and gets right past you. It was bump-head," he explained to Aoi, "and I'm the fool didn't know him."

The Combmaker came soon after that, fetched by one of the beggar's children. He was more intent and direct than ever before, with an underlying high energy that seemed to lift through his muscles, so that he moved lightly, continually confining springs of the knees and flights of the shoulders. He forced serious-ness into his face long enough to apologize for the beggar's failure to recognize that the priest was the man with the wen in disguise. "I am sorry if he frightened you," he ended.

"He frightened the woman," Aoi said. "She is wiser that we are. And Ateki was quite panicked afterward because she had opened the door and let him in." Ateki could still be heard crying in the kitchen, the woman soothing her with kind words. "But I was too puzzled at first to be frightened, then when he escaped it was quickly over. But perhaps now"—she paused to search her feelings—"I am not sure, but it may be that now I should be frightened." In her experiences on the road west she had known fear in so many varieties and gradations that now she must search up and down the scale to see if what she felt truly qualified for attention.

"Lady, when something finally frightens you, I think you will know it. Fear is not an emotion you have to look for. It comes out quicker than we like."

"You cannot teach me about fear. But don't tell me that you have ever experienced . . ." Then his eye rolled outward, his cheeks loosened into long lines, and she understood. "Forgive me, of course you feared for your family."

"Not enough. I wath not fatht enough with my fear, it wath not thtrong enough to take uth out of the path of priethts, alwayth fighting." He fell about, lolling on first one straight arm and then the other, his head turned away, miming dejection to disguise the depth of distress this memory caused him. Aoi waited, wondering how a person could talk safely with a man so injured by an accident of fate.

Finally he stilled, his emotion calmed, leaving him bowed in the shoulders, his face turned down and hidden. Then, "They have found you now," he said, "and either they think you can lead them to where the

minister is hiding or they fear that you know who
directs them. But we too are closer and it is true that
we know too much." Looking up at last, he recovered
his glee, the hard mirth of a man who fights.

"You have discovered something new?" Aoi said.

"Akimitsu . . . Ah, Akimitsu."

From his tone Aoi knew that he had found an
important proof. She waited while he decided what
misdirection would best help him prolong the pleasure of telling her.

"You know that Akimitsu has a house where no
minister's secretary should ever be expected to go?"
he began.

"Unh."

"It backs up to where a porter lives, no space
between, just a common wall. We saw him go in at
night, we saw him come out in the morning. We
followed Akimitsu to and from that house. But . . ."

He would not go on until she said, "Yes?"

"But . . . we didn't follow the porter who lives
behind."

"Why should you?"

"Yes, why? Except that the porter went into
Akimitsu's house instead of his own. It was early
dawn, barely light, that street was closer and he got
careless, thinking no one would see."

Aoi could not at once understand the significance of
what the Combmaker was saying. He saw her effort to
follow him and continued in a forgiving tone. "So we
began to watch the porter's house as well. Akimitsu
went into his house at night and soon after the porter
came out of the house behind."

Aoi held her breath.

"He walked along and others joined him until there
were four of them. They went . . ." He waited, hoping
she would guess the rest. But Aoi's imagination had
not quite caught up. "They went to the wall of the
mansion of the Minister of the Left, three of them
climbed over, and . . ."

"And the house burned. Are you telling me that Akimitsu himself . . .?"

"Ah, yes. He is that person also, that porter. And he burns and robs."

Just then the woman of the house came to say that the Combmaker was wanted at the gate. He left Aoi tangled in a confusion of images, trying to add another dimension to her idea of Akimitsu. But her thoughts flew too fast, she could not pause for refinements of character and motive. She had proof that Akimitsu participated in crimes. Was it not logical to suspect that, hoping to replace the Minister of the Right, he was also the one who had worked to have him removed? Exposing him was all that remained to be done. For that, she must go to the palace, rise again to a level where there was influence enough to dismiss him from his office. She must consult the emperor.

The Combmaker returned. "It is time to leave here," he said to Aoi, who was about to utter the same sentence. She nodded and called Ateki. "We have no carriage," the Combmaker was saying, "but one of my men is a public litter carrier and he will take you. You will go to the palace?"

"Unh." Aoi was forced to stand still while Ateki tied up her hair, but urgency made her fidget and before the last knot was complete she moved to the hall, a half-tied ribbon trailing on the floor.

So that she could enter without being seen on the street, the litter was set down close against the gate, its curtains folded up over the roof frame. Peering in, Aoi saw that the cloth on the cushions was worn and soiled. An odor of stale perfume met her, unpleasant but a needed shock to remind her that she moved in the world below the clouds. She settled herself, nodded briefly to Ateki, who would pack and come later in a carriage the princess would send to fetch her, and the curtains dropped. Beside the litter carriers, the Combmaker, the large beggar, and two of his equally large sons trotted as guards.

Under a leaden gray sky of late afternoon they started out, the litter rocking with the speed of the runners, the Combmaker's voice calling out as he cleared the way through throngs of walkers returning home. Aoi gripped the passenger straps and listened to sounds from outside: the calls of vendors, chatter and laughs from the crowd, and nearer, the steady jarred breaths of the men who carried her. A heavier grunt of breath was the first she knew of trouble. The next moment the litter plunged down on one corner, the carrying shaft breaking with a crack as it hit, throwing Aoi on her side against the tied curtains. Furious breaths near at hand and screams in the crowd accompanied the righting of her enclosed seat and she was flung forward as the litter dropped to the ground.

In the spirit of the chaos she heard around her, Aoi ripped away the ties on the curtain and sound receded as the dominant sense when the scene opened to her sight. The Combmaker, whirling a thick staff before him, retreated against the side of the grounded litter, threatened by a man in rough clothes who feinted and jabbed with a long knife. The beggar stepped into her sight and out again, wrestling a man who had attacked from the other side. Behind the litter, one of his sons lay bleeding on the roadway, the haft of a knife protruding from below his shoulder. In the background, people fled or huddled against walls to watch, strangely silent, not helping, faces full of the joy and terror of witnessing the breakout of violence among others.

Knowing herself to be the object of the attack, Aoi looked quickly to see how many came against them and identified five men with knives on this side alone. When she saw a sixth one, standing farther away than the others and fitting an arrow to the string of his bow, she let the curtain fall and turned to put her back against the front wall where he would not expect her to be, crouching as low as she could press herself and fearing the tearing agony of arrows. The struggles outside continued, now coming to her again as a confusion of shufflings and smothered cries.

Then there were new sounds—of wheels, the rattle of harness, hoofbeats, and a high voice screaming, "Ai, ai, ai!" on and on.

Had she looked, the Combmaker told her later, she would have seen a troop of guards in the uniform of the Minister of the Left and one of his carriages, Sukemasa leaning forward from the front opening, the sleeves of his robes flying backward, his black cap askew over one eye, his fist, when he could spare a hand from holding on, raised and shaking. The ox, the Combmaker said, overran two of the attackers who were driving against the beggar. Sukemasa's chant changed to "Strike, strike, strike!" and continued for several more cries after the fighting stopped. The guards with their swords and bows had killed three men and they arrested five, missing two or three more who ran away.

Aoi raised herself from her crouching position and by the time Sukemasa peered through the curtain, she had achieved a small composure and was massaging her arm where it had struck a post of the litter frame when it was dropped.

"The minister sent me," Sukemasa said to her.

For an instant Aoi thought he meant the princess's father, the minister she most wanted to see, the ever-dependable, all-knowing man who surely could not lose his power even when forced into exile. But confusion replaced her joy. The carriage she could now see bore the emblem of the other minister—who was ill, whose wife lay in a coma, whose daughter had died, who was left undone by multiple misfortune . . . and who was said to dislike Sukemasa. Even so, here was Sukemasa holding up the limp curtain of a public palanquin, barely clamping it between two fastidious fingers, his cap still tipped onto his forehead, his eyebrows soaring in disdain and exhilaration, mouth pursed. He said, as he had the first time she saw him, "Perhaps you were not expecting me, hm?"

Chapter 23

"How was it that Sukemasa came with guards just when I needed to be rescued?" Aoi asked the other minister. She sat with him in a room of the palace, amid piles of his possessions saved from the fire and the reek of smoke that rose from every article. The minister's usually full cheeks had slacked into flat planes and his eyes were almost hidden by puffed lids. In an adjoining room, his wife lay attended by her women, conscious now and occasionally moaning.

"Why . . . I had sent him to arrest you." The minister's pomposity was ragged but he puffed his cheeks and raised his chest. "Though I may not have lent my hand to actual governing in the past, it is all fairly obvious. One must have an agent, because after all one is famous and cannot go about just anywhere. And so one puts aside dislikes and aversions and chooses a man who can be used—to listen to people, to see whom they meet, where they keep their women, what stewards send goods to their storehouses, and where they go at night in unmarked carriages. Then when you need information from someone who is unfriendly, someone who is said to be hiding though we all thought she had gone into retirement with the departed minister, there is the very convenient power to arrest. I think I may say that in the short time in which I have had the sole responsibility of governing, I have mastered some of the simple principles much better than . . . Well, one must not be immodest."

"I had not thought myself unfriendly, a person who must be arrested and brought by force for consultation. If there is anything I can do for you . . ."

"You know where your lady's father is hiding in his retirement. Everyone says you are close to him, so naturally . . ." And with touching earnestness, "I have need of him. All this time, all this time of trouble and improper urgings, of change and perplexity that have destroyed my digestion, of f-f-f . . ." He seemed to be trying to say *fire* but that word would open in his mind the whole of the disaster to his family and it would not pass.

She spoke quickly to relieve his stuttering. "I would have come gladly, if I had thought . . ."

"But you would not have told me where he is, you are one of those loyal ones."

"Am I to understand that the government does not know where the Minister of the Right is at this moment?"

"He concealed his destination, everyone knows that." Aoi suppressed her breath of relief. The minister must truly have escaped.

"Now I say that you must tell me where he is offering up his prayers or I will . . ." Though he may have mastered the arts of secret agents and of arresting, the minister had no idea what tools of coercion he could wield against a woman with powerful connections.

The habitual tact of a lady-in-waiting moved Aoi to rescue him. "Oh, I wouldn't want that," she said. "And so Sukemasa was sent with guards," she continued. "And when he saw the Combmaker fighting around a palanquin, he knew that I was inside and needed help. Sukemasa was quite fierce, riding there in the front of the carriage."

The other minister was not interested in any surprising qualities Sukemasa might have shown. His face stiff, he said only, "There never seems to be anything Sukemasa doesn't know and he can be useful. But actually he is a very irritating man, as irritating as Genson—and that is probably why I thought of him to help me in this. He has done his job and we have proof that Genson is the one who sends men to set fires, create confusion, and murder us all."

"There have been many fires and it is true that people have died." Aoi paused to force darkness over the image of Miyuki but she could not entirely suppress grief and her voice caught as she went on. "But the intention in most of them seems to have been robbery."

He looked at her with pity. "Can't you see that now the intention is changed? He will do anything to get his man Akimitsu into a position of power so that he may dictate our lives. It is only I who stand in his way."

"You seem convinced," said Aoi, "that it is Genson who moves in all of this. But I see it differently."

"You cannot know how he has thought to force me." The minister's manner was intense, he leaned forward for emphasis, jabbing his thumb against his knee in a peculiar gesture of fury and rejection. "He was always coming to my house, dictating appointments, handing me new regulations already written."

"He left nothing to your own judgment."

"Exactly! Yes! I see that you understand." His brow creased, his lips pressed hard together as he forced himself to contain his outrage. "I began to think that he had persuaded the Minister of the Right to retire, and that he meant to remove me too."

Aoi considered. The minister must actually know

that the princess's father had been taken for banishment but it was convenient for him to pretend that his former partner had retired because of a willful desire to indulge in religious meditation. He would never admit even to himself that unjust exile could have been ordered in his name because secretly he had welcomed the chance to govern alone. By trying to find the absent minister through Aoi he was tacitly admitting failure. Determined ignorance was the protection and the set attitude of the other minister and she would only anger him by insistence on fact. She decided to make simple statements of the points of proof that there had been a conspiracy.

"There was an accusation of treason against the Minister of the Right, based on a forged letter."

The minister looked exaggeratedly bewildered. "I know nothing of a forged letter. But if there was such a thing, Genson has monks to do his bidding, skilled calligraphers. He must be stopped, he means to put his man Akimitsu"—his eyes closed and his voice sank and quavered—"who was my man, my faithful secretary, the one I trusted . . ."

"It is easy to be mistaken in men," Aoi said, to comfort him, but she would not abandon her project of setting forth arguments against Genson's guilt. "Those who attacked me just now, they were men of the city, hired ruffians." And there have been many of those, she thought, remembering the men who had starved and abused them on the way west.

"Exactly so. Genson is known to frequent the western city, and for what other reason than to hire criminals?"

"Sukemasa has said that he goes there?"

"His carriage is seen in those streets, a rattletrap that can't be mistaken. We too have our informers."

"I see." Aoi continued her listing. "The person who organized the fires and robberies always knew what valuables there were and where to look for them." She did not add that Akimitsu would have knowledge

of valuables and their storage places through hearing
the other minister recount his many visits day after
day.

"Just like Genson, to poke his nose into every noble
house. When he is called in for special prayers, he
manages to peep into all the cabinets."

Aoi lost patience. "You relate all these things to
Genson but I think that Akimitsu has hidden skills
and obsessions."

"Obsessions?" The other minister's face showed
clearly that he thought Aoi was being womanish, avid
for sensation and distastefully prying. "A man does
what he does, we don't need to know of obsessions."

"Indeed? And yet it is always helpful to find reasons
for what people do. Sometimes the only logic in
criminal acts is the warped reasoning of obsession or
blind desire."

He mouthed the phrase "blind desire" as he would
have expelled spoiled fish from his tongue.

"Someday I will explain to you my ideas about
Akimitsu," Aoi said. "But I say now that he is the one
who has directed these things."

"Impossible. He was always at my office, doing the
work of three men. I will send the Palace Guard to
find Genson and hold him. Then all this will stop and
my friend . . ." He paused, mildly surprised that he
had used such a word in referring to the Minister of
the Right, toward whom he had always felt guilty and
defensive. Then he nodded, affirming to himself that
the two of them had complemented each other and
that he would gladly see his partner take up the
responsibility of governing again. "My friend can
return and everything will be as before." But just then
his wife cried out behind her curtains and, even while
he smiled at his vision of the stable future, tears
tracked wetness on his face.

With effort, he sat up and gathered himself to
discipline Aoi. "You have too much imagination and
you have fastened on Akimitsu quite unjustly. It is
Genson, I tell you, who is reaching out from his

temple to set Akimitsu in a high place where he can be
manipulated. It is Genson who went to the western
sections to meet his criminal friends. He actually
went into a house and talked to them, absolute proof.
A man like Genson does not go to such a place except
for the worst kind of purposes."

Seeing that he was not reasonable on the topic of
Genson, Aoi abandoned argument. "Your Excellen-
cy," she said. "Let us wait awhile and bring both
Genson and Akimitsu together. There is one aspect of
past events that should tell us which of these two men
leads the other." She told him of her secret visits to
the emperor to treat his eyes, and of the theft of her
medicine chest. "So much has happened since the
early morning fire at the princess's house that the
strange reason for that crime has never been considered. But I am convinced that they meant to stop me
from curing His Majesty, that they hoped to remove
his influence by forcing him to resign, if some worse
fate did not intervene. Let us do it this way." She
spoke to him for a long time and proposed a test of
Genson and Akimitsu that would determine which of
the two was a criminal. They would require the
emperor's participation and they went together to see
him and arrange for a meeting of the council on the
following day.

Since it was late in the afternoon, Lady Omi was
still with the emperor, giving him the day's final
treatment. The chamberlain, the same one who had
customarily admitted Aoi, greeted her with smiles
and asked them to wait. The anteroom was strangely
empty, no others waited to see their sovereign.

"I had heard, lady, that you disappeared when the
Minister of the Right was sent away," the chamberlain said. "I take heart for the future to see you here
again and seeming"—he looked carefully at her face,
knowing the conditions she must have endured and
searching for any inner damage—"seeming un-
changed. You have done great good to His Majesty by
sending this competent lady to him. Giving the treat-

ment twice a day, since she was so nearby, seems to have speeded the cure. His eyes are almost healed, his strength and resolve have returned."

"And I heard," said the other minister, "that you had been relieved and promoted into retirement. I was against it myself," he added, "but there was talk that you had lost your manners and offended a few councillors."

"Fortunately one cannot be retired in such a way just on the whim of high officials. I protected the emperor in his illness and he refused to let me go." Such a statement from a man like Sukemasa would have been accompanied by simpering and smug solemnity, but this chamberlain spoke matter-of-factly and with simplicity. He was one who would someday be a councillor himself, rising past the Fifth Rank of retired chamberlains.

The emperor wore a dry bandage across his eyes, to rest them and to preserve as long as possible the effect of the blue crystals. But he was erect on his cushion and his voice flowed steadily, with none of the hesitations and dyings away that had marked his speech in the depths of his weakness.

Aoi let the other minister explain that they needed to summon a full meeting of the council, with Akimitsu and Genson both present, to be held the next morning. He detailed, with offhand deference to Aoi, her plan for proving the guilt of the person who had been the organizing force behind the robberies and fires and the instigator of a possible plot against the minister who had disappeared into retirement. The emperor suggested that the councillors be summoned separately, each one thinking he was asked to visit the emperor. He feared that if a full council meeting were called, they would be afraid to come and send excuses. He also suggested several deceptive embellishments that he could add as he played his part and Aoi left the two of them dictating to the chamberlain the notes that would go by special messenger to all involved.

She left the palace just at dusk and she was reminded of her last visit here and the strange sounds that had come from the old Court of Abundant Pleasures. Now that proofs were falling into place, she thought she knew why that court was said to be haunted and she went toward it, intending to investigate. Low clouds were blowing in from the west, trees and shrubs shook and quivered, black in the shadows. Figures in the distance hurried with flapping robes. As she reached the path that led across the north end of the building, a single crow, wing feathers spread, cut its untidy flight above her shoulder, cawing almost into her ear, so that she dropped into a crouch on the gravel and stayed there as the whole flock rasped cries of alarm and flew off to a farther tree. Tiny drops of rain, driven hard, stung against her skin.

Sitting on her heels, sleeves billowing, face turned to receive the weather, Aoi felt rested and blown clean. The brief fright caused by the crow had released other frights—for the abducted minister, for the emperor, for the success of the test of Akimitsu and Genson—and, as if they had been hard flat seeds, those fears were now taken by the wind and sent sailing. She had become a shell, air turning and sweeping within as it did on this deserted garden walk and she touched the end of a twig to anchor herself. It was acceptance. She had done what she could. From now on all of them would be moved by the power of events. The world was, perhaps, after all, a good and natural place and what would be would be. She had only to continue her existence in the clear light of reality and she would walk into her own future, recognizing and at ease in each landscape as she came to it.

Footsteps scraped the stones behind her and she moved to stand. But the old monk, who stopped, facing her, waved her back and she stayed as she was. He wore white clothes and a basket hat that shadowed his face. Motioning toward his throat, he indicated to her that he denied himself speech. With his hands he blessed her and she knew that, because of her position, his eyes regarded her full form. Everything in his manner added to her peace.

Just then, as she still crouched on the path, as she watched the old monk walk into the windy gloom, the sturdy push of his legs oddly unmonkish, she heard a high shriek from the building beyond the hedge. It was not the same kind of chittering sound she had heard before; it could not possibly be human, but an empty building does not shriek by itself. That other time she had not gone inside but now she rose and walked through the gate, up the weedy and broken stone steps, across the outer gallery, through trash of leaves and brush to the ancient door. It slid back surprisingly easily. In a trance of curiosity, she entered.

Bats flew over her head through the open door. The hall reeked of their droppings. To the right she could see a line of columns, darker struts of darkness that dwindled into the depths of the far end. And there sinking and flaring as the wind moved, was a light, showing the feet and legs of several men shuffling and straining at extreme angles around a cube of solid black.

Hands up to tear away cobwebs and fend off the bats whose flight she could sense but not see, Aoi moved forward. The black object scraped along the floor, making again the high scream she had heard outside. Intent, giving no thought to her own visibility, she paced steadily nearer. Her outer robe that day was of a deep autumn bronze, but the underneath divided skirt was pale blue and reflected light from the wavering flame. Before she could understand what these men did in an unused building on the palace grounds, they perceived the floating advance of ghostly lighted cloth and scattered, some out the farther door, some into invisibility in the left-hand corner of the hall, leaving the oil light in its basin on the floor. Aoi, transfixed by her conviction that these men were thieves shifting stored goods and by association of this fact with the fires and robberies, realized too late that a curtain across the corner hid those men who had not run away and that they had come out along the wall and were now behind her. She was just turning when a voice said, "Now, little brother!" Light exploded in her head and she fell.

Chapter 24

The next day carriages came and went at all the palace gates, as the members of the council arrived where they had been told to enter. Nearing the emperor's private residence, each one was surprised to see others walking in the same direction, but chamberlains and ladies-in-waiting appeared and politely prevented their retreat.

Genson stepped down from a cart so old that its plaited palm-leaf sides were black with damp and mold. He was attended by a young page in rich temple clothing that was of noticeably fine quality and a bevy of monks as ill-dressed and solemn as Genson was himself.

Akimitsu came on foot from the office of the other minister. Though he had no contact with the man he served, he still used his old office and he still sent a stream of proposals to the minister, which were always returned without the official seal. The government had continued to run through secret agreements between Akimitsu and the secretaries of most of the other ministers. Some of these secretaries walked with him, conferring until the last moment. He left them outside and entered the palace alone. He wore robes of brocade, dark blue in color but so sumptuous in pattern and thickness that even the highest lords, eyeing him as he approached, coveted them.

When they had all collected in the main hall, they looked around and realized that the entire council was present and that they had been tricked into a meeting. Sorting themselves by rank as they sat down, none of them would sit near Akimitsu. The fact that they had had to depend on him in recent weeks, that they knew he had built a vast mansion and wondered where he got such income, the persistent fear of choosing sides and distrust of his ambition made the councillors wary of him. The Minister of the Left also would not have him near, though usually he needed his secretary at his elbow. Several councillors tried to shunt him to a position of low status at the back of the crowded room but he resisted their maneuvers and took a place beside Genson at the front but with a wide space between them.

Though this hall was a small place for so many men, behind the raised platform where the emperor would sit when he arrived, folding screens had been set to close off the end of the room, further limiting the space. The members of the council who had to sit so close together thought that the emperor's women, whom they presumed were behind the screens, could have been left out of this business, whatever it was, in which they would have no say.

When the emperor entered he wore a broad white cloth over his eyes and his movements were feeble. Two chamberlains led him with discreet pressures and helped him to sit on the raised platform at one end of the room. The assembled men were hushed, except for the sound of indrawn breaths. He sat until there was absolute quiet and then began to speak.

"I despair," he said, and was silent for such a long time that there were small movements of puzzlement among the seated figures as they waited. "Illness . . ." He seemed to lack strength to complete a sentence, but heavy phrases followed one another, with separations between them. ". . . has unstrung every purpose . . . set vital parts in revolt against each other . . . enfeebled the strengths of health . . . fevered the processes of repose . . . cast off the balance of dual vision . . . attacking from within. Why has this happened? Is it punishment for bad deeds?"

Murmurs of denial swept among them but no one voice dared speak positively of the emperor's reign. Genson set the theme. "Your Majesty will always be remembered as an upholder of tradition, never lax in self-discipline or in care for his people's spiritual health."

More and more audible comments on remembrance emerged and then died down as the emperor prepared to speak again.

"I am accepting of the will of heaven but I must not neglect the resources of man and I have decided to make an appeal to all of you, the wisest in my realm. You have learning and experience and is it not possible that there is some cure for my trouble that is known only to some special one of you? If any man can name a cure for me, he will deserve to be set above all others and the rest of my days will be spent in giving thanks." He referred to the post of Prime Minister, an office that ranked above those of the Minister of the Right and of the Left. It was not always filled but was sometimes given to exceptionally able men and was now vacant.

Understanding that the emperor was announcing his intention to retire, the men murmured again but no strong voice emerged to speak against his departure. The councillors knew that only Akimitsu and Genson dared expose opinions.

Akimitsu, with impassive face, spoke formally. "We hope not to lose the benefit of your wisdom." He referred to the wisdom of a retired emperor, which could be sought or ignored. One finger of the hand spread on his knee stroked a curve in the raised design of the blue brocade.

Genson, with his fiercest piety, said, "Karma is not to be escaped. Yet it may be that I can offer a cure, one I would have described long ago if I had been consulted." He broke off and beckoned to one of the monks he had brought with him. "Prepare some ink and write this down for His Majesty."

The monk drew from his robe a portable writing box and a sheaf of paper. He laid a cloth on the floor in front of him, weighted the corners of the curled paper on top of it, arranged his implements, dripped water onto the stone, ground the inkstick back and forth, and uncapped his brush. Every man watched these deliberate preparations and silence stretched out, so that when he was ready, Genson's intoned prescription came like an oracle from a god.

"Take the fresh skin of a lizard which has been living in a temple and lay it on the affected eyes for a whole night. This must be bound closely, so that no light is allowed. Then the lizard's quickness will enter the eyes. In the morning bathe the eyes with water from the holy spring at Kiyomizu and the sacred water will wash away the disease. Of course, all participants in the ritual must have fasted and prayed in preparation, and there must be no women in the whole building for a day before and a day after the ceremony. Women, Your Majesty, cause many pollutions."

A man in the back began to laugh and Genson turned a stony face to see who it was. All were silent but there was the rustle of shifting and rebellious movement.

"Shouldn't there be medicine?" someone said. "I have heard"—his voice rose with enthusiasm as the possibility of becoming Prime Minister, with a huge income and unlimited influence, worked in his mind—"that a poultice of willow leaves—"

Others from all over the room began to suggest remedies used by their old nurses, their mothers, the ancient wise men of their households.

"Surely you understand," said the Minister of the Left, "that we cannot risk harm to the emperor with untried medicines. We will not agree to any treatment unless the prescriber can show me a written history of its use. And of course, the man who suggests the medicine must first use it himself."

The councillors, though educated in Chinese history and literature, had no knowledge of even the most famous medical scrolls. Several of them proposed to set their scribes to searching for appropriate writings but they were silenced by the confident dourness of Genson's glances. He said, "I can show you at least ten instances of miraculous cures in the records I have." He turned toward Akimitsu and almost smiled.

Akimitsu had so far made no suggestion. But the arch assurance in Genson's manner caused his cheeks to flush. He turned away, put his hand up to adjust the collar of his outer robe where it crossed in front, fingering delicately along the lush folds. Seeming to ponder, he faced the emperor with such gravity that every man was quiet. For seconds he did not speak but it was obvious that he was gathering resolve to oppose the bitter monk who, they all thought, had sponsored him.

"With respect," he said in a low voice. "But lizard skins and holy water have the flavor of magic."

Genson's voice in reply was muted by deep shock. "You do not respect religious inspiration and ancient holy practice? You do not believe in divine revelation? You do not accept the wisdom of years of study?"

Akimitsu ignored him and spoke again directly to the emperor. "Surely all the power that religion can muster has already been used for Your Majesty's benefit. And we see you now, after months of suffering, not at all improved. Let us be more pragmatic, let us try concrete means, ancient, yes, but not mysterious."

He paused to let murmurs from the assembled men rise and fade again.

"And have you," the emperor said, "a cure in mind? One that is documented and safe?"

"From my father, the former emperor," said Akimitsu, "I inherited a small but potent library, including many rare scrolls and parts of scrolls, some written in a language I take to be Sanskrit. These I cannot read myself, but the ones in Chinese, no matter how ancient, are accessible to me." He bowed slightly to the emperor. "You know how thorough is the education of princes."

Murmurs arose again at this reminder of his lineage. He waited, in an attitude of respect, still turned to address the emperor.

"One of these scrolls I have read many times. It is a treatise on medicine by the Chinese sage—ah, I forget the name but your doctors would recognize it. He suggests the touching of certain blue crystals to infected eyes. The cure is certain and absolute."

"I see," said the emperor, and he made a sign to the chamberlains who sat near him. They left the platform and went behind it, where they began removing the folding screens, revealing not the emperor's women but the Minister of the Right, Lady Aoi, Sukemasa, and a troop of red-coated guards. Two of the guards sat on either side of a tall, heavy-limbed man dressed in rough clothes. His arms were bound and he looked at Akimitsu, opening his mouth in a pitiful attempt to speak. Others of the guards ran to wrench Akimitsu from his seat and search his clothes for a weapon, but that day he had been armed only with the costly, deep-textured silk. He rose tense in the hands of the guards, straining toward the dumb servant from his house in the porters' quarter of the city.

The crowd of councillors watched this drama without understanding its meaning. There were uncertain

movements toward the door, the beginnings of
shouted cautions for respect, and cries that the exiled
minister had returned and that he sat there before
them. The emperor, blind behind his bandage,
showed no surprise. When he reached to untie the
cloth, every man was still. The emperor revealed eyes
that were bright with health, that swept musingly
from face to face, recalling to each man's mind his
behavior when the Minister of the Right was taken
and the government faltering.

The Minister of the Left glared first at Akimitsu,
then at Aoi, who had predicted this result. She was
bowing to the emperor as she moved to sit far to one
side, the councillors near her shifting away to avoid
any appearance of association. Most fiercely he glared
at Genson, whose chiseled face had relaxed into
simple dismay. Whatever it was that had happened
here, Genson's influence was ended and the minister
intended that he should understand that. Then he
regarded his companion minister and began to weep
with joy.

"Forgive our deception," said the emperor. "But
life has been rather dull and discouraging for me these
last months. I hope to make the point that my health
has returned, as has my able Minister of the Right,
and that we intend to heal the ills I spoke of, the fever
and loss of balance in public life, the revolt and
enfeeblement which have afflicted us all."

The Minister of the Right, who had sat down at the
front of the room, looked over the crowd with his
usual placid detachment, not accusing, not injured or
self-pitying, but observing as he always had whatever
was before him. Aoi, remembering how he had rescued her the night before, was not yet struggling to
suppress the expansion of feeling that sang through
her. He had seen her go into the old Court of
Abundant Pleasures because he—disguised as the old
monk who had blessed her—could not resist turning
for one last look at her, sitting in such a simple
attitude on the path, her robes lively in the wind, her

hair lifting and falling behind her. He had seen her walk entranced into the thieves' storehouse and he had followed and frightened away her attackers.

Akimitsu, who had been forced to his knees, pulled away from the guards and turned to face the minister he had thought to kill by mistreatment on the journey west. His robes had become disarranged and he grasped the collars on both sides and pulled violently, as if to rid himself of the encumbrance of elegance or to free his arms for action. The guards held him. No longer controlling his features, he screamed one word, "How?"

The Minister of the Right, amused now, answered, "Ah yes, how did we get away? Your men were city men, they should never have allowed themselves on a boat."

Akimitsu, who had himself never been on a boat, did not understand. The minister explained. "You took them from several places, I think, so they did not all know each other. Some of them were men who enlisted to protect me and these few influenced the road taken, so that we came to the coast at a village on one of my oldest estates. There we went on shipboard to cross the sea to Kyushu. This lady was dressed as a fisherman's wife and taken away, though our guards thought she was shut up in the cabin. Then we set sail and wind and waves did the rest." The minister smiled but not deeply. "Seasickness leads men to forget their duty. They were easily overcome. Some"—his voice became dry and he turned away— "may even have fallen overboard. I imagine that those who survived did not dare return to you."

One of the councillors raised his voice. "We see before our eyes that this worthy secretary is arrested. But why? For offering a cure for the emperor's eye disease? What has he done? Why is he suddenly pulled around in such a disgraceful way?"

"It was Lady Aoi who cured my eyes," the emperor said. "She used a treatment involving blue crystals, which is described in a certain scroll of Chinese medicine, a treatment kept secret because the doctors disapprove of it. Her scroll was stolen when the princess's house was robbed and set afire. This person"—he would not say Akimitsu's name—"knew the cure, so he must have read the scroll after it was taken."

"But he says it came from his father's library."

"As it did!" said Akimitsu, flexing his arms in the grasp of the guards but held fast.

"I suppose that is possible," said the minister, "but knowing the cure is not the only proof. Do you see this other man? He is a laborer with his tongue cut out and he was taken from a house in the porters' quarter. He is Akimitsu's servant, the house is Akimitsu's house, where he went almost every night. It was because he knew this poor servant that Akimitsu betrayed himself. From that house he recruited men and sent them to rob and burn. Sometimes"—he looked at Akimitsu, weighing his capabilities—"you went with them, I think. As on the night this lady's scroll was taken. None of your men could read, you had to be the one to look for medical writings. All the stolen scrolls, the lady tells me, were richly wrapped except the crucial one, which was of simple paper and not obviously valuable. Ordinary thieves would not have taken it."

The servant, though he could not talk, showed by his amazement that all this was true. The council subsided.

The other minister, feeling left out, entered the explanations. "Genson," he said, and Aoi feared he was off again on his favorite theory, "has mixed himself into this trouble from the beginning, though his predictions may have been honestly made at first. He has talked, lectured, chided, dictated, disapproved, and been utterly lacking in sympathy. But we see him as he is, a stringy morose man who hates comfort because he hates himself." The other minister, in his passionate dislike of Genson, did not realize that his perceptions had deepened and that he was describing the same kind of inner qualities he had scorned as unwholesome probings in Aoi's explanations. "Ah, he allows himself the pleasure of a boy but he thinks he shouldn't and that makes him more bitter. All this is perfectly plain. But this one"—he flicked his hand toward Akimitsu—"this one deceives. He seems loyal but takes advantage of his position. All his life is split. Who is it that lives in the retired empress's old mansion? The boy who hates women, the man who neglects his wife. Who builds a fine new mansion? The government servant who expects to rise through treachery, who has secret income from thieving. Who lives in a poor house among porters? The criminal who enters where everyone sleeps . . ." The other minister's voice died in his throat. In the anguish of his losses, he had adopted Aoi's explanations, which were confirmed by what he had seen in this room. Now he knew that what she had pieced together from small intelligences gathered by the Combmaker and by Sukemasa was a constellation of facts. By setting out her theory publicly, he raised it to the status of truth, with the air of telling the obvious. If he was convinced, anyone should be, was his attitude.

The councillors looked sideways at one another and fiddled with their court fans in embarrassment. The other minister's descriptions of Akimitsu's concealments made them uneasy because they could not imagine a personality of such complexity. "Give us some proof, tell us that he was seen setting fires," they said.

"I myself have seen him in the clothes of a porter," said the Minister of the Right, "and I will tell you quite simply what this man has done."

He had compared notes with Aoi during the long night before, when they had gone to Lady Omi's room, knowing they could depend on her to receive them without exclamation and to keep the secret of their return. It had been important that no one except the emperor should know that the minister was at the

palace. Lady Omi took him a message at once, then
left them alone to talk throughout the night. They had
agreed that he would make all the explanations today
because Aoi wanted to conceal as much as possible
her role in the proofs against Akimitsu. It was always
her desire to be unremarkable, to retain the freedoms
of an ordinary woman.

"Akimitsu took an interest in one of my daughter's
ladies and visited her in my house. There was an
evening when it was hot and I took off unnecessary
clothes and sent them to my room before Akimitsu
came to call. On his way to the lady's room that night,
he took my official seal and put a forged one in its
place. That was the beginning. I knew the next time I
used it that my seal was changed but I could not
understand why and I waited."

He glanced at Aoi. "There was a curious thing
about that lady he visited. She was actually his wife, a
woman he had married to gain property when he was
quite young. He came upon her again by chance in the
market one day and he was drawn to her without
knowing she was the girl he had abandoned years
before. I imagine she was quite changed.

"Then came the forged letter. You spoke of your
education," he said to Akimitsu, "but you didn't
mention that you learned to imitate the writing of
others, there in that provincial schoolroom. You
wrote that letter, just as you wrote Chinese lessons to
win favor with the provincial lord's dull sons and
false wine chits in the lord's handwriting for your
farmer friends."

Akimitsu, seated among guards, did not react.

"So I was sent off, and Lady Aoi with me, because
you knew from reading her scroll that she was curing
the emperor. You had taken her medicines but still
she was a threat. How ambitious you were to remove
everyone who might be in the way of your rise into my
place."

He sighed. "It must have seemed that you would
succeed. I was gone, the emperor was sicker than ever,

you were rich from selling stolen goods to the provincial lords who so long for articles of culture from the city. And you had Genson to cry doom and to prod the other minister about your appointment. Then you found out there was someone who knew you, knew your ways with other people's writing and your habit of forming bands of farmers' sons. That person was your wife. What a shock it must have been. She, on the other hand, had recognized you from the beginning. She was afraid of you but she could not resist the chance for revenge and she rejected you just enough that you would be challenged and come back to be rejected again. She never answered your notes, did she?"

Akimitsu's eyelids sank lower but he did not move.

"Some people cannot mind their own business," the minister continued, "and such a one sent you one of your wife's poems, to console you for her coldness. You recognized the writing she had been so careful not to let you see. How swift you were, how efficient. My daughter was invaded again, this time in my house, and the lady was found dead after the fire, a sword through her heart."

The emperor put out a hand to stop the recital of evil deeds. "It is enough. We need no more proofs."

The council buzzed and roared with talk. "It is not for me," the emperor went on, "to decide punishment. But I will make a suggestion. Let us confine this man to the old mansion of his grandmother, where I am told he ruled with pitiless misbehavior in his youth. Let us say that his wife may live with him—but I think she has probably already left. Let us ask for men and women to serve him and see if any will volunteer. And let us guard every gate and patrol every wall, to keep him there. He is an emperor's son but he will live like the poor porter he made himself into. Do you agree?"

Not one man dissented.

Epilogue

"It is heartbreaking," the princess said, "that we must all return to houses that are burned. It is too desolate, I cannot . . ."

"Don't upset yourself," said the prince. As soon as the Combmaker sent word that his father-in-law was safe, he had left his odorous hiding place in the lacquer shop, stopping first at the house of a widow friend, who had very pleasurably assisted him to bathe and had replaced his clothes, scenting them all with a perfume she knew he liked. "I am here now, I will to see to all that," he said to his wife.

She moved her eyes to a spot on the floor just short of the cushion where he sat. Anger and dependence balanced up and down in her feelings and she had not yet looked at him, though he had been with her for a day and a half, because she could not decide if he had saved himself or deserted her. She thought to keep him in suspense.

"It is plain, though," said her father, "that we cannot all stay here at the palace. These rooms are small and meant only for temporary residence. The other minister has already moved his wife to a house lent him by his cousin. Lady Aoi and I will go tomorrow back to my house."

"Father, you cannot take my lady from me at a time like this."

Lady Omi said, "We can send for Lady Takumi . . . And perhaps someone will help us find a new lady."

"I have a young woman in mind," said the prince.

His wife turned her back. The scale was tipped.

The minister, unperturbed by his daughter's protest, said only, "I must have her with me."

At the edge of Aoi's mind a small void of denial opened against the dazzling emotion that had filled her since the minister's return, because it had been so stunning to come to her senses there in the old hall and find herself safe against his chest as she had been so many times on that awful journey, to feel the bulk of his arms and the rise of his breath. Fever does not last, she said to herself, one either dies or recovers. But first the heat must run its course.

Sukemasa, who had come to visit, raised his peaked eyebrow but was too well-trained to allow the titter that disturbed his throat. He said, "My house was so small that what should have been a minor fire has destroyed it entirely. May I serve you, sir, in some way?"

"Not in my house," the minister said rather too quickly. "I have larger duties in mind for you. Why don't you report to the crown prince's household. He could use someone who is experienced in the ways of the court to give him a little polish and teach him that grace and dignity are virtues."

"But this young royal person cares only for games and hunting. He heaves himself around like an ox, begging your pardon, and has not a grain of sense in his shaggy head."

"Exactly. You are to apply your sharp aspersion and bully him into caring for his clothes, using his morning wash water, practicing with the brush until he can write respectably, that kind of thing. But if all that is too much of a challenge . . ."

"Bully . . ." Sukemasa said in a faint voice, his eye fevered with imagination.

"You have his father's permission."

"Hm," said Sukemasa, nodding.

Aoi left with the minister as planned. It was O-hana, her maid, who exhibited a shy and demure manner, while Aoi matter-of-factly checked that her precious box was among the luggage and entered the carriage with no attempt to hide her face. Rain fell all that day and Aoi the minister sat at evening beside a round brazier.

He sighed. "I promised myself that I would retire from the world. There was a temple they took me to before we got back here and for days I would not leave. With so much to do, so much trouble to counter, such pressing need to return to the city and help, I could only sit in a room behind a blind, braziers on either side of me and one behind, and watch the angle of the sun in the dying garden. A bush warbler sat on the same branch every evening and sang, so I thought, just to me. The simple temple food of beans and noodles was ravishing, the thin bed could have been heavenly lily pads, I drank pure water sip by sip, it was such nectar. I could not see this as attachment to the world, an improper enjoyment. I had been in the world, it was a rough place not to be admired, and I felt I must find faith again in the possibility of good."

"But still you left," she said. "To take up your duties."

"Ah yes, duty. All my life I have done my duty and I don't know now if it was because I thought I must or if I did it for the pleasure of doing, of being involved. I didn't think about why—it was my life and I lived it. But now . . ."

"We were thrown out of our normal lives and that changed our perspective. Over and over again I remembered with longing the feel of the princess's morning basin of hot water—warm molded silver against my palms, the sway of weight as I carried it, steam in my face. It seemed the essence of what we had lost, of calm domestic arrangement and civilized living. Yet I used to be annoyed when I had morning duty and I never thought about that bowl of water except that I was sure to spill it."

"I would have welcomed such memories but I was not able to escape the awful present of that journey. Such misery among the farmers, such ignorant brutishness among our guards. Where had I failed in my duty to those people? If the ruler is good and the government is good, the people should be contented and happy people. We have laws against excessive taxation but they have been evaded. Had I been blind, I thought, seeing only my own estates and thinking them normal? On that trip I saw all around me my own failures."

"And for a while afterward you wanted to give up," said Aoi. "That is only natural, you had been starved, wounded, and ill with fever. You had no strength left."

"You are right. And perhaps it was as strength returned that conscience moved me and finally I left the temple. I lived as a begging priest, though the Combmaker provided me with a warm place to sleep." He stirred the charcoal with long bronze firesticks. "I have no hope left," he said. "The world of the city will go on with its meannesses great and small, absentee landlords will starve their farmers with illegal taxes, women will be married for profit, and children will grow up without love. But I am one man who has seen these things and I must try, with the power given me, to help." His smile as he turned to her was serene. "Soon, soon," he said.

Aoi breathed in. He had in mind only an interlude with her, he would not press her to stay. She felt a little ashamed to be relieved.

"All through that awful journey you never complained," he said. "And since your escape you have been working alone, yet you never gave up," he went on. "I serve my emperor, I love my daughter. But when a man is struck down, it is not the pull of his own obligations but the courage of another that raises him."

"I only asked for reports and received them. And I was not alone, I had skilled help."

"It is my thought that if I am not with you, you are alone."

"Yes," was all she said. For the moment it was true, and who was she to decide the future?

In the house of the minister's head gardener, a small girl played with a toy her father had given her. It was lumpy and brown, polished now by the child's hands to have highlights of pale bronze. "Poor sheep," she called it, and she had a habit of cradling it in her hand and crooning to it. "Poor sheep, poor sheep."

"Why do you say that to a piece of stone?" her mother asked her.

But the child could not explain.

It was cold in the temple room where Genson lived because he would not allow himself the luxury of a brazier. After he fell asleep, uncovered as usual, his young page took a quilt from the pile on his own bed and pulled it over the stiff form of the monk. He did this every night and he knew that Genson trusted that he would and that his master's sleep was pretended. The boy lay down again and within minutes heard the even breaths of true sleep. Then he left his bed and the room, lifting the door as it slid, a skill he had learned early in his residence there.

The fat carriage man slept in a small space in a corner of the kitchen and the page went there and shook his foot until he wakened. "Well, well. The young one." The man's sleepy voice had a growling quality. He did not sit up but lifted his arm and peered under it, instantly awake and composed. "You think yourself important, since you came back."

"You went out today." The boy was calm.

"Yes?"

"And came back with another bag of gold for the secret closet."

"Ah. So you have found even that."

"From now on you will give me a share, just as you take a share."

"Is that so? And why should I do that?"

"He doesn't know that you are dishonest."

The massive weight of the carriage man rolled to sitting position, his breath heaving as he pushed himself upright, his voice held just below a bellow as he said to the boy, "I serve him as no one ever has and you come here, sneaking about at night, you spying little . . ."

"You take a dip from every bag of gold dust." The boy's voice did not rise, he did not change his easy sitting posture. "You have a whole fistful of your own by now and you keep it here," and he touched with delicacy a place between the man's legs where a worn leather bag dangled from a strap. "He is strict, he would be angry," the boy said.

Choking sounds in the throat were all the expression of rage the man allowed himself. "Your parents have put you up to this," he said. "You went home and told them . . ."

"I went home because it was the only place I could go to get away from him. And I don't tell what I know or you would be . . ."

"What are you, only ten? And already so vicious? You think you can report on me, don't you know I can . . ."

"He would not believe you. I am only a child, as he was. But soon he will need a younger boy and I don't intend to stay here. With gold I can live until I become known as a scribe."

"Ah well. I see that he has taught you that if there had been gold he would never have had to come here. And I don't know why *I* need it. I will probably die right here in this hole because I will never leave him."

The mansion of Akimitsu's grandmother seemed from outside almost normal, but in the grounds the paths became clogged with blown leaves and no one swept them away. Leaves sank into the edges of the pond and floated on its surface among the remains of lilies. Inside the rooms were dark because in only one of them were the rain doors ever opened. Here Akimitsu lived.

He had gathered about him the best articles of lacquer, scrolls, folding screens, writing boxes, and standing curtains from the whole house and they lay piled at the edges of the room, until there was space in the center of the floor only for a set of bed pads, which were never removed or aired. Wine bottles lay everywhere.

When he left the room, he always took his sword. The old woman in the kitchen, who was the only servant in the house, would hide in the storeroom because it had a wooden door and could be locked from the inside. She would hear him run into the garden, where he slashed at the weeds and plunged about on the sandy paths. Or if he stayed inside, he ran through the corridors, stabbing into the paper of the sliding doors and hacking at cypress pillars. The old woman was afraid of him but she remained because she had never until now been warm in the winter or had dependable meals, and the storeroom held treasure enough to barter for charcoal, food, and wine for the rest of her life.

The Combmaker lay drunk in his shed in the market. He had seen Akimitsu bundled into a carriage by the guards and had intended to follow, but just then Genson had passed through the gate in his battered cart, holding the boy page by the shoulder and concealing his own face. That was enough to let the Combmaker understand that never again would Genson summon the council to hear his predictions or call in high places to leave his written edicts for strict living. Genson was a monk who had made himself conspicuous as a caution and an example for others. If he was hiding now people must know that he had no more influence.

The Combmaker caressed his wine jug and mused on the future. The Minister of the Left will send rich rewards, the prince will send robes and incense, the Minister of the Right will give me a house or some such extravagant thing, he thought. But what would he do with clothes and a proper house? Sell them all for wine, drink all day until he fell down, seeing visions of rioting priests and making his dream hand hold weapons—knives and swords, a tall bow and far-traveling arrows. And his aim would never miss.

Throughout the city artisans devised ways to make blue fish, always small and secret articles. Within a week of the return of the Minister of the Right, a new fashion became apparent among poor wives for wearing against their skirts clusters of tiny glass fish strung on thread, which had long ago been marks of authority in China. One of the fish was always colored a strong blue. Tiny blue cloisonne fish-shaped boxes were ordered by aristocrats anxious to indicate their partisanship when they took them out from among their clothes to extract a pinch of dry perfume, and the more worried men of the court wore thin strips of blue ribbon painted with gleaming scales fastened among the streamers on their hats. Children played with wooden fish dyed blue and lost them in the grass beside ponds and lakes. After a while, when the Minister of the Right had proposed laws that threatened to cut the income of half the court, the fish symbols were put away. But certain vendors, beggars, and carpenter's helpers had secret tattoos of blue fish on their arms strong and weak and remembered with pride how they had come from nowhere to rescue a minister and a lady.